The guy was the school brainiac. My sister's crowd. *Not* mine.

Just ask him out! my friends Dev and Olivia told me.

Ha. "If it doesn't work out, my sister and all of her dorky friends are going to know!" I cried to them. "I mean, can you imagine getting dissed practically in front of the entire nerd patrol?"

Thing was, the minute I'd seen Charles's face, it was like I'd been zapped. I just *had* to get to know him. "I just wish there was a way I could figure out if he was likable before I did anything," I said to Dev and Olivia, looking back over toward Charles's table in the caf, where my sister was pursing up her face like she'd just eaten sour grapes, literally. "And somehow I don't think my sister's going to be a really neutral source of information."

Brainstorm. Then again, maybe she would be. . . .

His. Hers. Theirs.

The Popular One

LIZZIE SKURNICK

BANTAM BOOKS
NEW YORK · TORONTO · LONDON · SYDNEY · AUCKLAND

RL: 6, AGES 012 AND UP

THE POPULAR ONE
A Bantam Book / October 2001

Cover photography by Barry Marcus

*Produced by 17th Street Productions,
an Alloy Online, Inc. company.
151 West 26th Street
New York, NY 10001.*

ISBN: 0-553-49374-4

Visit us on the Web! www.randomhouse.com/teens

Published simultaneously in the United States and Canada

Bantam Books is an imprint of Random House Children's Books, a
division of Random House, Inc. BANTAM BOOKS and the rooster
colophon are registered trademarks of Random House, Inc. Bantam Books,
1540 Broadway, New York, New York 10036.

PRINTED IN THE UNITED STATES OF AMERICA

OPM   0 9 8 7 6 5 4 3 2 1

To my very own sister, Miriam Julia

One

Ebony

REMEMBER SLEEPOVERS?
I don't mean the just-you-and-your-best-friend kind of sleepovers. You know—you rent *Pretty Woman, Cruel Intentions,* and *She's the One.* You eat two packages of low-fat Hot Pockets and three pints of double-chocolate mocha crunch. You see who can stick her stomach out the farthest. Then you collapse into bed, except you don't go to sleep for three hours because each time one of you says, "Okay, okay—now we're *really* going to go to sleep," the other one is only silent for three seconds, then starts giggling and screeches, "But did you *see* those pants Erika was wearing in biology?" and then you have to scream about that for three more hours until you realize your best friend hasn't said anything for a while, and then you realize the *reason* your best friend hasn't said anything for a

while is that she's snoring into her pillow, and then about four seconds later you're snoring into your pillow too.

Not *that* kind of sleepover.

No, the kind of sleepover I'm talking about is the kind you had in fifth grade. Your invitations had balloons on them, or stars or a rainbow. (You had to invite all the girls in the class—your mother made you.) When they came over, you had a scavenger hunt or played charades in the living room. Then you had pizza. Then you got into your pj's and pretended to go to sleep, and you read the dirty parts of your parents' books to one another until your mom and dad finally came down the steps for the fifth time to yell at you to be quiet and you realized they were serious, they really would send everyone home, so you shut up, and you fell asleep—unless you were the kind of girl who asked, "Ebony? Are you awake?" across all the other sleeping bodies, in which case you went into the kitchen and ate more of the cold pizza with your friend, giggling at some girl's bunny-feet slippers, then tried to be quiet when you went back into the room and stepped on someone's arm and woke everyone up.

No, I'm not in the middle of some big term paper about sleepovers. I'm asking this only because I'm fifteen, and my twin sister, Ivory, *still* uses the invitations with the rainbows.

Okay, I'm kidding about that part. (She just e-mails everyone, when she isn't going crazy with

2

the color printer.) But by seventh grade I had out-grown those kinds of sleepovers. Obviously by the time we both started high school at Roosevelt, I thought my sister would too. And maybe Ivory would have if she had ever torn herself away from her chat rooms and alt.rec whatevers long enough to come downstairs, have a spoonful of coffee-toffee crunch, and discuss the cuteness of Ryan Phillippe's butt.

You're getting the picture, aren't you? That Ivory's captain of the math, science, and chess teams (which, coincidentally, have all the same members)? That her favorite after-school snack is a peanut-butter-pickle sandwich? That because of a certain plastic headgear that she favors, she's known—informally, of course—as the Headband Queen of Roosevelt High?

That's right, folks. It's all true.

By the way, my name's Ebony. *Yes, as in the song.* We're twins, and we're named Ebony and Ivory. Don't start ragging on me about Michael Jackson and Paul McCartney, though. My parents named us *one full year before that song came out.* My mother is black, my father is white, and they are impossibly deluded people who thought that it would "impart the spirit of brotherhood" (Dad—hello? We're sisters?) and "make people think" (that's Mom). Whenever they repeat that to us, Ivory always responds: "Yeah. Make people think that our parents are weird," and Dad tells the story for the millionth time of how he grew up with triplets named Dit,

3

Dot, and Dash, and that if we had any common sense at all, we would thank our lucky stars to be two such pretty girls with such pretty names.

The Dinner Table,
    Following the Above Argument
MOM: [*satisfied smile*]
DAD: [*happy look at the three of us;
puts arm around Mom*]
IVORY: [*eye rolling*]
EBONY: [*eye rolling*]

Anyway, that's one of the two things about which Ivory and I agree. That and how we never, ever want to hear the story about how my parents met (at a party in Brooklyn), dated, got engaged, and were married (the day before Christmas, in three feet of snow), ever, ever, ever again.

You might wonder why I started telling you all this. Maybe you think I just like to talk a lot. (True.) Maybe you think I'm the kind of girl who complains all the time about her family. (True—but I love them all a lot. Kind of.)

The truth is, I started telling you all this because I have a big, big problem. I need my sister's help. And the fact of the matter is, I'm about 156 percent sure that the Headband Queen of Roosevelt High isn't going to exactly be of said help.

Okay, I'm gonna start at the beginning. Like I said, my name is Ebony. I'm a sophomore this year, which is great because to be honest, freshmen at

Roosevelt High are mighty low on the food chain. And while Ivory's idea of a good time is to stay home with a mug of root beer and her Kaplan SAT workbook, I am obsessed—*obsessed*—with movies. Especially anything starring Ryan Phillippe.

Obviously I am big in the drama club. I guess you could say that I'm something of a drama queen. In fact, my two best friends, Dev and Olivia, say that all the time. Example:

```
    A Typical Scene in the Cafeteria
EBONY: [holding back hair to show mas-
sive zit on forehead] My life is over!
DEV: Eb, gimme a salt, will you? [grabs
salt]
OLIVIA: [chewing]
EBONY: [grabs one of Dev's Tater Tots
and gets over zit]
```

It's funny how Dev and Olivia and I are so close, actually, when we're all so different. Especially since Dev only came to this country (from Israel) when we were all in seventh grade. Olivia and I had been friends since first grade, and when I first became friends with Dev, that caused some tension. But by the time we were all heading toward eighth grade— our last year at Jefferson Junior High—I was more worried that Olivia and Dev were so close that they didn't need *me* anymore, not that I was going to have to choose between *them*.

Lemme just tell you about my best friends for a

sec. Olivia is the kind of girl who is so perfect in every way that you want to hate her, but she's so cool, you can never get around to it. First of all, she's gorgeous, with long black hair, almond eyes, and a teeny, size-one figure. (Olivia's Vietnamese, and teachers always do a double take at her adopted name, MacDougal, when they see the girl it belongs to.) As long as I've known her, she's always gotten straight A's in every subject—not because she's a grind, really, but because she's read every book ever published in the world, practically. She's also an amazing poet, and she's been winning writing contests and awards at school as far back as I can remember.

Dev—short for De-*vo*-rah—is about as opposite from Olivia as you can get in every category. First of all, she and her family emigrated from Israel when she was thirteen, so she has a really low, throaty, accented voice in contrast to Olivia's so-soft-you-have-to-ask-her-to-repeat-everything murmur. She's about five-ten to Olivia's five-one, and her head is surrounded by this enormous crackle of sun-streaked, curly hair. Instead of reading poetry, Dev is always swinging her lacrosse stick or sliding into second. (Even though we're only sophomores, there's a rumor that Dev might be picked for volleyball captain this year since she spiked and served out more games last year than I can count.) She also loves everything junk foody: whenever Olivia chides her about her food choices and offers her a minicarrot, Dev just rolls her eyes and takes a bigger bite of her corn dog.

6

Really, though, when I think about it, the biggest mystery isn't why they're friends with each other, but why they're friends with me. Because while on the outside they look very different, actually, both Olivia and Dev share a lot. They're both incredibly private and very stable; not given to flights of fancy, crushes, or delusions; and they both keep their rooms incredibly neat.

But guess whose room looks like—as my dear old mom would say—a bomb hit it?

Anyway. I didn't mean to go off on a big thing about my friends and my life. But I guess you need to know all this background if you're going to understand anything about my problem with Charles.

You didn't know my problem had a name, did you? But it totally does.

Charles Corey.

It all started (just like it always seems to) in the cafeteria.

I just have to acquit myself of a couple of things first. I know I must seem like the kind of girl who would always have crushes on guys. But I'm not that way—seriously. In fact, not counting Ryan, I only had a crush on one guy all through junior high. His name was Jason Warshof, and I did all the stupid things you do when you have a crush on some guy who doesn't seem to notice you're alive: put him on your buddy list, hang around his locker even though your next class is two floors away, laugh way too hard at his stupid jokes at parties.

I guess Jason must have noticed me eventually,

though, because at the end of last year he suddenly asked him out. (Secretly, I suspect that Dev or Olivia must have leaked my crush to one of his friends, and he only asked me out because, after all, what guy wouldn't want a girl with a crush on him hanging on to his every word?) Unfortunately, he overestimated my crush—or rather, I overestimated *him*. After two dates it was clear that Jason had only two topics he could converse on: baseball and baseball. And my crush went down the drain faster than a spoonful of Comet.

I say this only so you don't get the idea that I get some hugola crush on every new guy that passes through the doors of Roosevelt High. (Although there is always something extra cute about new guys, isn't there? Why is that?) My feelings about Charles Corey are—I swear—totally unprecedented.

This is exactly what happened:

   A Typical Day in the Cafeteria,
                  Scene 2
DEV: Right, Eb?
EBONY: [*silence*]
OLIVIA: Ebony, what are you looking at?
EBONY: [*silence*]
DEV: It's like she took a zombie pill or
something.
EBONY: [*silence*]

I don't remember this part at all. But this is what Olivia and Dev told me. That Charles Corey walked through the door of the cafeteria. (With Peter Enright, the school's biggest nerd besides my sister. But I didn't notice that then.) That I stood up like someone possessed by the posture demon, then sat down just as weirdly. That I didn't say anything for a full five minutes.

The part after that I remember.

Of course, after I snapped out of my daze, I had to get all the dirt on him that I could. I mean, like, *immediately*. Luckily Shannon Dunn, the biggest gossip in our grade, was sitting right across from us, drinking her normal three chocolate milks and holding court with all the most popular girls in our year.

I beat it over to her table like the Dallas Cowboys were stampeding behind me. (It was only Olivia and Dev, wondering what strange force had taken over their friend.) I slapped my palms down on the plastic tabletop and looked Shannon straight in the eye. "Tell. Me. Who. He. Is. And. Do. It. Now."

To her credit, Shannon didn't even bat a eye. Looking from side to side first, she grinned happily and leaned forward to whisper the news. "I hear he's, like, a *total genius,* especially in math."

I leaned back, too afraid to look in the direction of the guy who was hotter to me than Ryan Phillippe + Benjamin Bratt combined. He was somewhere in the left-hand corner of the cafeteria now—I knew; I could feel it. He was a genius? "Like, Rain Man genius?" I asked tentatively.

Dev crossed her arms. "Will someone please tell me what is going on?" she growled.

Shannon shook her head. "Maybe if you would get your head out of your catcher's mitt," she chided.

Dev's face darkened. "Maybe I'll put something else in my catcher's mitt," she began. "Like your face."

Olivia jumped in before Dev stopped Shannon from ever gossiping again. "I think . . . um . . . maybe Ebony has a little crush?" she explained, jerking her head ever so slightly back toward Charles, whose name I didn't even know yet. *"Don't look!"* she hissed, placing her hand on Dev's arm before Dev could jerk her head around.

I love Olivia—she is *such* a stealth bomber. "Exactly," I whispered to Dev, putting my hand on her other arm.

She shrugged us both off. "Can I look now, Your Highness?" Dev whispered back sarcastically. (By the way, if you haven't figured it out yet—Dev thinks boys our age are a lot less useful than a really good pair of cleats.) Shannon giggled again, and I shushed her.

"We can all look when we walk back," I said. Dev turned and went first—not really on my orders, probably, but because she was bored. Then Olivia. I was about to go when I remembered something. I leaned down to Shannon again.

"What's his name?" I whispered fiercely.

Shannon grinned again. "Charles Corey," she said slowly.

Charles Corey.

I'm not going to bore you with all the stupid details, like how Dev and Olivia totally agreed that he was cute after I asked them eighty-seven times, how I spaced out so much during chemistry with Mr. Rosner that he asked if I had mistakenly inhaled some fumes, how I looked through the halls desperately for Charles the rest of the day and didn't catch a glimpse of him *even once.*

Needless to say, the math genius was not in any of my classes.

Because that's not even the bad part. The bad part happened when I got home. Actually, when we sat down to dinner. Ivory and I had made our typical it's-our-night-to-cook meal: lasagna, garlic bread, and salad. We were all chomping down when the phone rang.

Ivory jumped up and got it, putting her palm up to Mom's "No phone calls during dinner!" shriek. "Uh-huh," she said into the receiver, chewing methodically. "Uh-huh. Uh-huh. Okay." Then she hung up and sat down without indicating in any way who she had been talking to.

"I would like you to listen to your mother when she tells you to do something," my father said in the deep baritone he reserves for not-yelling-yet. Ivory shrugged and stuck her fork deeply into the heap of pasta. (It's not that Ivory's rebellious or anything; honestly, I think her mind is in Deep Space Nine so often she has no idea when Mom or Dad is even peeved at her.)

11

"So, we've got some new genius guy named Charles for Big Think," Ivory said as if no one had said anything, adjusting her pink plastic (*pink plastic—did I mention?*) headband.

I almost had a heart attack. Obviously, instead of paying any attention to my family, I had been planning all sorts of tricks and gambits to get to know Charles—things like dropping my tray in the cafeteria or somehow getting ahold of his schedule and hanging around the door of all his classes. (I know: stalker.) But I got a fearsome shock at the words *genius* and *Charles*. How many new geniuses named Charles could there be at Roosevelt High? Clearly Ivory had beat me to the punch.

Before I tell you about the rest of the debacle, I should explain about Big Think. It's basically, like, an Olympics for dorks. Schools from all over the tristate area come and compete for scholarships. The winning team members get ten-thousand-dollar scholarships each and a fifty-thousand-dollar grant for the school. Our school always sends a team made up of the highest scorers in math, English, social studies, science and technology, and history on this test they give us right after Christmas break. (Believe me, it was just *thrilling* to spend a whole week of mornings taking each section last month.) We've even had some individual winners in past years. But get this: there's a Big Think club made up of kids who just practice all year round—for *fun*.

Of course, Ivory is an avid member.

So after Ivory dropped the bomb, Mom and Dad forgot all about her answering the phone during dinner. Mom smiled, like she always does when anybody mentions a boy. Dad put his head down into his pasta with renewed enthusiasm. And then Mom said the dreaded words:

"Was that him?"

I got so nauseated, I almost fell into a *swoon*, right there at the kitchen table. Oh my God. What if my new crush had just asked out—my *sister*?

Ivory never talked with her mouth full. We all had to wait for the garlic bread to go down.

Ticktock. "Well?" I prompted with a little too much force, cementing the probability of my mom sniffing out my crush.

Ivory shrugged and turned back to her food. "No."

Suddenly I could breathe again.

"It was Mr. Rosner," she continued. "He was just saying that with *Charlie* joining the team and all, we'll be putting in extra practice sessions on Thursdays and Fridays now. *To get the most out of him*," she spat.

I might have been totally consumed with dreams of Charles, but I wasn't blind. My sister wasn't *my* competition in a fight for Charles. Clearly my sister was competing with Charles herself—for the captain's seat at Big Think.

Was that going to make it harder or easier to meet him?

Mom and Dad stayed oblivious, as usual. "That's great," Mom said. "I hope you'll let Mr.

Rosner know that we'd love to have everyone over for pizza if you run too late."

Ivory smirked. "Oh—I'll be sure to do that," she said.

The gears in my brain started whirling like those plates showmen spin at carnivals. If Charles came, Ivory would lock the team in the study for hours—even if I traipsed around in full makeup and a ball gown, he would be oblivious. I could start going to Big Think meetings myself, but after the amount I'd made fun of Ivory for her dorky after-school projects for years, she might become radically suspicious at my sudden interest. In fact, she'd probably *figure out* the reason. Which could be potentially embarrassing. Dangerous, even.

Despite her name, Ivory wasn't above some minor-league blackmail.

What was I going to do?

"Ebony? Ebony?" Mom was saying. I jerked back to the kitchen table like I had been slingshot from ten thousand light-years away. "What? What?" I stammered.

Mom smiled that disarmingly kind smile she always uses when she's vowed to get to the bottom of something. "And what did you do today in school, dear?" she asked, spooning some more lettuce on my plate.

Of course, I was so freaked out that Charles was already a big topic at my dinner table, I didn't answer her. I was thinking about how I'd have to ask

Dev and Olivia about what to do. Whatever was going to happen, I didn't want a repeat of Jason Warshof. I was going to get to *know* him first this time. But without exposing myself to too much humiliation.

And for that, I needed a plan.

Even if Charles was the king of all the Big Thinks at Roosevelt, he wasn't necessarily going to want to hang *out* with those dorks, was he? I mean, he'd practically be *living* with them in the weeks before the meet anyway. Wouldn't he want a separate social life in the form of—say—me?

I had another thought. *South Pacific* auditions were coming up next week. So I'd be living in the auditorium with the rest of the drama club until opening night. So if Charles was glued to Big Think and I was glued to the play, when would we ever meet?

"Ebony?" Mom prompted again, her eyes widening. I'd spaced. *Better answer quick,* I thought, trying hard to look like I was just bored out of my skull from all the Big Think talk.

Which normally would have been totally true.

"I don't know," I said to Mom, popping a grape tomato in my mouth, making sure not to spit all the seeds across the table at Dad. I shrugged, looking at Ivory, close lipped as usual. Well, two could play at that game. Somewhere, somehow, I must have inherited an ounce or two of Ivory's self-control, even if I couldn't really feel it ever. "Stuff," I said, chewing with my

15

mouth open so Mom would switch the conversation to her second-favorite topic from boys: manners.

"Ebony," Mom said, frowning. "Now, really."

"Sorry." I chewed.

How was I going to make sure that Charles Corey was someone I *really* wanted to know—before I even got to know him?

Two

Charles

IMAGINE IF EVERY day you woke up and you had a completely different life.

Your room was different. Your clothes were different. You went to school, and your school was different. You had new friends. The car your father picked you up in—new. The town you drove around in—different. Even the money you used—sometimes it was different.

Some things stayed the same. Your mom and dad were the same people. They worked in the same jobs. They had the same types of friends, who talked to you as if you were the same age that they were. They had the same kinds of dinner parties, events, meetings. And you had the same computer in your room and your row of old books and writing notebooks. Your same straight-A report card, even if the name of the school always changed.

No, I haven't been watching a lot of old *Twilight Zone* episodes. I'm just trying to give you an accurate sense of the life of Charles Corey.

The lifestyle my parents lead could be referred to as *peripatetic*. According to my trusty old *Roget's Thesaurus*, it could also be called *nomadic, bohemian, itinerant, restive,* and *vagabond.* That's *vagabond*, from the Latin *vagabundus*, meaning "strolling about," or *vagari*, "to wander," which, incidentally, leads us to *vagus*, the root of the word *vague*.

Are you getting the picture? Probably not. As my mother sometimes says to me, I often use my intellect to *obscure* the world, not explore it.

I'm a genius. All right? I'm not being conceited—believe me. At this point I truly think of it as more like a third eye or having blue skin—something that sets me freakishly apart from every kind of group I'd like to be a part of.

A trait that I'd be very, very happy to lose.

I'd give you the abridged version of my life, but I'm so sick of having to tell it to people that I'm thinking of printing it up on cards. I must have told it to hundreds of other kids. Thousands. At more schools than you even knew existed.

You see, my dad's a genius too, but in a very different way. He's an inventor. I know how you all think about inventors: the crazy man down in the basement with a shock of hair like cotton candy, surrounded by tubes and vials filled with weird-looking stuff, who burns off his eyebrows every other week with another huge explosion. Well, that's not my dad at all. (He doesn't even have a study at home. He likes—get this—any kitchen table. Sometimes at other people's dinner parties, when he gets an idea, he'll wander off and use *their* kitchen table. So far, we've been able to keep him out of restaurant kitchens.)

I guess he is kind of weird looking in his own way, though. (But what dad isn't?) He's really tall and thin, with long arms and huge hands that make him look kind of like a crab. He has about eighteen pairs of the same brown corduroy pants that he wears with different T-shirts all the time. I think that's just because Mom got sick of trying to make him wear anything else, though.

You see, nowadays when you're an inventor, you don't labor in the basement with a bunch of cardboard boxes for company. What happens is you get hired out by corporations. Big, fancy corporations. Who pay you piles of money to just sit around and think up stuff.

How did my dad get into this racket? you must be wondering. (And how could you?) Well, it usually happens by accident. With my dad, it was before he even went to college. He was working as a gofer at a small paper in his hometown, Birmingham, Alabama, getting coffee and running copy from the newsroom down to the printer. One really hot day, the printing press got broken. My dad was hanging around, and he asked if he could take a look. They must have just let him look at it for a laugh—what could the fourteen-year-old gofer from the newsroom know about a big, huge old printing press, after all?

Except my dad fixed the problem. In ten minutes. Then submitted a design for an addition to the mechanism that would—and did—increase production by fifty percent.

End of story.

Except it wasn't, at all. He made a gabillion dollars from the patent to that addition, and other companies called him in for consults. Since then he's designed so many things, I can't even keep track. Gadgets to increase all fuel efficiency. Production. To blast off from the moon.

Since you ask, he didn't design Post-its, though. I think that was some really smart nongenius.

My mom's kind of a genius too, I guess—in an entirely different way, though. She's a musician. She was trained as a concert pianist, actually, and as a teenager she achieved a little fame in the Midwest, where she was raised, winning all kinds of contests and awards. When she was seventeen, she went off to Juilliard, the big music conservatory in New York City, to study. The story is, she was accompanying her friend on a very difficult Schubert *lieder* (that's "song," to all you non-classically-trained singers) when she corrected her friend's intonation by singing the section back to her. (See, this is what happens when you know

20

too much about everything—you have to explain things all the time. *Intonation* means, in a general kind of way, how close you are to the right note.) After hearing my mom's voice, the teacher had a hissy fit, basically, and insisted my mom start studying with her. And after that, my mom was a singer.

When I was little, my mom used to let me look through all her old scrapbooks, from performances she did in London, New York, Paris, Ontario. (Singers go wherever anyone's willing to listen to them, my mom always says.) She wasn't as famous as Leontyne Price or anything. But she's famous enough that wherever we move, someone's mom or dad has always heard of her and drags out the old record they have of this or that performance and makes her sign it.

Or—if she's in a really good mood—sing it.

That's how my parents met. Mom was in Florence, studying with some really famous teacher who, Mom says, used to rattle the double-paned windows whenever he corrected her "interpretation" of a certain section of a song. And Dad was studying how to make plastic molds for kitchen implements set faster for some Italian manufacturing plant. (Really.)

That brings us to the moving thing, though. You see, Dad basically has a waiting list of corporations who want him to work for them. Whenever he's bored or finished with a project, we move on. You might think this would irritate Mom, but it doesn't. Even though she had kind of a career in the making as a singer, she always had terrible stage fright. She hated performing, actually. So she was really glad to finally be able to give it up and concentrate on playing the piano, which she truly loves.

And which she can do anywhere we go, as long as the piano comes too.

This would all be really great, except then my parents had me. So now, instead of two happy people wandering around in the yard thinking up how to land on Mercury and humming Mozart at 2 A.M., it's three people, the youngest of whom thinks his parents are really cool but wishes they could just sit still for a second.

Because the thing is, whenever Dad and Mom move, I have to move too. So now that I'm fifteen, I've been to something like twenty-five schools. And this is where the not-wanting-to-be-a-genius thing comes in. Because if I didn't already know most of the course work they hand me in any class—if I couldn't already speak four languages fluently or teach advanced probability to a class of seniors by myself—if my grades started to go down, for instance—why, then my parents would have to settle down and let me get my stuff together, wouldn't they?

Wouldn't they?

Then I might have a chance to make friends with someone other than the principal. (That's the other thing about being a genius—principals are always really nice to you because they think somehow you're going to make the school famous. The thing I want to know is, how am I supposed to make the school famous if I'm only there for two months?) I'm sure you can really imagine what having the principal suck up to *you* does for your social life. Honestly, sometimes I think my mom knows more kids at the schools than I do since she's always teaching five or six of my fellow students.

She's probably more popular than I am too.

Yeah, so, why do my parents even make me go to school if I already understand everything? If I get straight A's almost without thinking? If I could basically watch VH1 fourteen hours a day and still get straight 1600s on my SATs?

Get this: because they want me to have a social life.

Don't be jealous because homework's really easy for me. If I had known that knowing calculus at the age of nine was going to guarantee the fact that my best friend was my computer screen wherever I went, I would have hit my head with a hammer and fixed the problem a long time ago. Or pretended to be stupid, which (I think) a lot of kids already do to fit in anyway.

You see, being a genius doesn't even mean that you can really *do* anything. (Except after you've done something really cool, when everyone else just decides you're a genius and says so. Like with my mom's singing.) Officially, it just means you've taken a lot of tests and your IQ's really high.

Here's my own personal theory: Being a genius doesn't even mean you're smart. It just means you're *quicker*. Let me explain. You see, ever since I was little, I've been able to understand stuff. Faster than other people, I mean. For example, my mom and I would be shopping at the grocery store, and I'd give her the total a few seconds before the cash register came up with it.

I guess that wouldn't necessarily be that weird. Except I was only two years old.

Or Mom would start singing along to some aria from an opera that was playing on the radio, and I would sit down with her at the piano and start playing along.

Again, that's not really all that weird. Or it wouldn't need to be. Except I was only three years old at the time, and she'd hadn't even started teaching me piano.

The way I think about it, other people can add up huge lists of numbers, right? And millions of people know calculus. The thing that sets me apart is that I understand a lot of stuff just—automatically. Like, the math teacher writes an equation on the board, and I just get the answer in my head. I don't even really have to write it down to check it. It's like my brain does it faster than I could write it down anyway.

Some people think all geniuses are like Rain Man. (That's been my nickname at about every school I've ever been to—I think people forget the was, um, autistic.) But I can't do any of that weird stuff that that Dustin Hoffman does in the movie. I couldn't count a stack of cards by just looking at them. I couldn't start reciting prime numbers into infinity without even thinking about it—I don't know if I could do it while I *was* thinking about it. And neither can my dad. It's just, I'm like him. I can look at a thing and right away understand how it works.

What I can't do is what my dad gets paid for—picture how to make it *better*. That's really cool—that's a real *talent*. Like my mother's voice—it really does sound as beautiful as they write in all the old reviews—"like a shaft of sunlight," one reviewer said. And this girl at one of my old schools, Sarah—she wrote these poems she used to read in English class that made me *shiver*. Or being able to paint so that something looks realer than real—I can't do that at all.

How is just knowing the answer to a question anything special? I mean, it's not like I had anything to *do* with it. I'm just *getting* it.

Like a cold.

This explains why it's Monday morning in Somewhereville, and I'm about as thrilled to be attending my new high school as I would be to be covered with some really itchy rash. Actually, a rash would be great. I'd take a rash over another new school any day of the week.

Why doesn't Dad ever get job offers at places where you could scratch for credit?

For a first day at any school I always try to dress kind of low-key. Having a genius father and an eccentric-singer mother has given me some clues in that direction, at least. (No flowing emerald green caftans or T-shirts with No Dumping Here emblazoned on them for me, thank you.) For my first day at Roosevelt High, I was just wearing chinos, a white T-shirt, hiking boots, and a jacket.

A blend-in outfit.

I'd already seen the school. The previous Friday the whole family—me, my mom, and my dad—had all gone in to meet with the new principal, Dr. Guess. He was okay, I suppose. (He looked like every other principal in the world—bald, eager, caffeinated.) Of course, he'd seen all my transcripts and was thrilled to "have me on the team." (His words.) He started spouting all this stuff about my student teaching a bunch of courses and perhaps doing SAT prep for the upperclassmen, but my mom totally shut him down. (But in this very quiet, polite way, so he almost didn't notice.) She's really cool about that, actually—she's very hyped on my having a "true adolescent experience," whatever that is.

Unfortunately, however, Dr. Guess didn't stop there. He started talking about the "Big Think"—this student-brainiac meet they have in this area, where all of the schools compete for scholarship and prize money for college. Mom's eyes lit up.

"And you'd like Charles to become involved with this?" she asked excitedly.

It wasn't about the money. Dad gets enough from all the inventions and patents to send me to college fifty times over. (I have almost half my college credits done already anyway—a lot of the schools I've gone to have just given up on me and sent me to do "independent study" at local colleges.) I knew what was making Mom so thrilled.

This was an *extracurricular activity*.

After-school stuff has been a big bone of contention between me and Mom for years, actually. Ever since I was five, she's been yelling at me to join band, photography club, the newspaper, whatever. And I've been yelling back that I don't want to join anything when I'm going to have to quit it before I even have a chance to do anything.

In fact, one of the reasons we've been fighting so much is that I *did* have something I liked doing two high schools ago, and I was really mad to have to quit it. It wasn't an after-school activity, exactly, but it was close.

Dad was working with a baseball team in Modesto, California. (Don't ask—I don't think even he understood what he was really supposed to be doing.) And there was another girl like me—a "genius," I mean—at the local high school.

Mary Claire was very cool. She had read more than anyone I've ever seen—her parents had converted the garage into a library for her since she'd

27

already filled up the downstairs, upstairs, garage, and attic with her books. It had shelves and everything, like a real library, and whenever I went to find her, she was always sitting in an old beat-up recliner out by the garage, reading one of her thousands of books.

Mary Claire was a "novelist." (The quotes are hers, not mine.) She had written one of every kind of novel: westerns, romances, mysteries, sci-fi. She'd even done some imitation "Russian" novels, in the style of Pushkin.

Her entire closet was lined with her manuscripts, which she doled out to me like they were some highly controlled substance. "Corey," she'd say, standing at the door and clutching the manuscript to her chest. (She always called me by my last name.) "Treat this as if it were your own."

What Mary Claire didn't know for a couple of months is that I really did. Treat them as if they were my own, I mean. Her novels were so incredibly good, I was really scared to tell her that I had a stack of manuscripts—screenplays—that I'd written on *my* closet's floor.

When Mary Claire finally found out, she was furious. "Corey!" she sputtered, holding all ten of my spindly screenplays in her arms, her freckles standing out against her skin, she was so angry. "I can't believe you've been holding out on me!"

I could believe it.

Ever since I've been little, I've loved movies. I don't really believe in picking favorites, though. If you really pushed me to the wall, I would say my favorites are *Cool Hand Luke, To Sleep with Anger, Fargo,* and *Murder by Death.*

This week.

My mom's a big cineaste too, by the way. (Movie lover, to all you bibliophiles.) I think that's how I got the bug. When I was little, I would always try to stay up late with my parents, watching whatever they were watching—like everyone does. Then my dad, who gets bored by movies, would go to bed. And I would snuggle against my mom, hoping she wouldn't notice that I was still up and send me to bed too.

Eventually I guess it got so that I wanted to stay up for the movies themselves, not because I didn't want to feel like a baby. My mom would drink a glass or two of red wine and I would eat yellow raisins, and we would stay up until midnight, watching movies on the old classic channels. Then the credits would roll, and Mom would turn to me with brimming eyes and say, "Charlie, wasn't that beautiful? Now get your narrow behind to bed."

But just because I'm a genius, that doesn't mean I can write, does it? I mean, I've always had all these scenes—all this dialogue—that I've had to get down. The words just spin in my head, like mobiles. But having an urge to *do* something doesn't mean you're any *good* at it. You only have to hear my dad try to sing to know that.

But once Mary Claire got her hands on all my

scribblings, that all changed. "Corey," she breathed, barreling into my room the next day (M.'s a really fast reader, of course) and waking me up from a dead sleep. *We have to do something with these right away!"*

To be honest, at first I thought that Mary Claire was a bad dream and that she'd come to set my screenplays on fire. That about sums up my state of mind on my literary and dramatic capabilities, thank you very much.

"M.," I remember saying (I always call her "M."), "are you completely out of your mind?"

Well, M. had all these crazy schemes to send my work out to contests and searches and stuff. I pretty much put the kibosh on all of that right away. What we finally settled on was that M. would do dramatic readings of several key scenes in all my stuff, I would videotape her, and we would edit the work together and smooth it out.

That worked out pretty well, for a while. M. had all these crazy hats from her mother that she liked to wear, and if she was playing a male character, she'd put on an old Groucho Marx glasses-mustache-nose thing, then whip it off to play the girl.

Actually, it was the most fun I'd had in my life. Until we moved. Again.

That's why I knew Mom was so psyched about Big Think—she was thinking that this would be a real opportunity to meet other students who were smart, who were interested in the things I was. Who could *replace* Mary Claire.

"So even though they've been practicing all year," Mom was asking Dr. Guess, her eyes shining like fish scales, "Charles could still join the team?"

Dr. Guess was practically rubbing his hands together. "Oh, I'm sure Big Think would be thrilled to have an addition like Charles!" he drooled. "It's a team activity, after all," he added.

"Yes," Mom agreed, much too vehemently.

So it's a team activity, I thought. *But they're already a team.*

Dad alone emerged as the voice of reason. "Don't"—he coughed, like he always does when he's saying something negative—"you think that the other students might resent Charles coming in at the eleventh hour?"

Mom and Dr. Guess both looked at him like he was Ebenezer Scrooge at a Save the Children fundraiser. "William, really," Mom said, and left it at that. Dr. Guess nodded like she'd just completely summed up what a complete, total idiot my dad had been since time began.

"Big Think will be thrilled to have Charles," Dr. Guess said, standing up to shake hands with both my parents and me. "I'll *personally* guarantee it," he added, looking like he would run a tank over anyone who got in his way.

Oh, now I'll really go over big! I thought, trying not to grimace as Dr. Guess tried his best to pop all the joints in my arm. *I'm a mental genius, not a physical genius,* I wanted to crack. *If you want to show your love, why don't you rub my head?*

Dr. Guess must have heard me with psychic mind vibes because he *did* give my head a violent rub as we finally left.

"Now," Mom said, taking my arm as we left the main entrance and entered the sunny parking lot, "you'll have a chance to make some *more* friends."

She didn't say the words *Mary Claire*. Mom, Dad, and I had already had enough big fights about them making me leave the one real friend I'd ever had in my life behind.

"All right, Blanche," Dad murmured. "Let it lie. Let it lie."

What my parents didn't know was, I wasn't being agreeable because I had suddenly seen the virtue in my mother's arguments. I was being agreeable because (*a*) I was sick of fighting with them, and (*b*) I had a secret plan that my parents didn't know about.

I first saw the pamphlet for Rush Creek at a library where I had tutored kids in math after school, two or three high schools ago. In fact, the pamphlet was half hidden by a row of SAT and PSAT workbooks, behind which I could just make out the beginning of the school's tag line:

Make Your Own Way

I pulled it out to read the rest:

in the World.

It wasn't just some stupid summer program designed to make more money for the school and keep kids out of their parents' hair, I realized as I read. In fact, it was something I'd never really heard before: a kind of "college" for kids who couldn't stand everything about high school.

I had taken a lot of college courses before, obviously. Of course, it sucked. There I was an amusing oddity, like a talking cat or a bearded lady. The regular-age students had two reactions: they either treated me like a *wittle* baby who they had to coddle or like the evil spawn of Satan. To tell the truth—I preferred the second one. There's only so many moms a guy can take, especially when he already has a pretty active one.

But this wasn't some creepy think tank or some nursery school for kids who couldn't cut it. In fact, it was incredibly hard to get into—out of five hundred applications a year, they took twenty kids. And it wasn't designed for losers or outcasts. It was designed for students who were ready to concentrate on something—dance, trumpet, composing—*now*.

And it offered scholarships.

Looking at the amazing list of visiting speakers and faculty in the past couple of years, I got incredibly excited. Here was a place where other kids went when they needed more freedom to work, not more discipline. Where I could do my own writing. Where I would be pushed instead of coddled.

Where I wouldn't be some big freak to everyone else.

So last fall, when my father informed me we would be moving *again* the following spring, I did something I'd never done before in my life.

I *applied*.

And that's why I was being so agreeable about the Big Think thing. If everything went well, I would get a letter in a couple of weeks telling me I had been accepted for the next fall's semester.

And my *vagabond* days could come to an end.

By the way, Mary Claire and I still e-mail all the time. Every day, in fact. Now I know what it's like to have a real friend. Someone you can actually talk to about stuff without them thinking you're a dork or without you thinking that they would be better off buried to the neck in a field of other potato spuds.

To: CoreyFlakes@erols.com
From: Pebbles507@aol.com

C.—
   I bet you're in a snivet. But you should just suck it up and appreciate all you have. Do you know what I would give to get to travel around all the time, like you do? To meet all those new people and see all those new places? Why don't you try to enjoy it for once instead of being a big, stupid loser?
                     Your BF,
                     Ms. Mary Claire

You're probably thinking M. and I must have had a romantic relationship. I mean, we were best

friends for a while, right? And we were both geniuses. It should have been some huge match made
in heaven.

I guess I forgot to mention a really key fact about
M. Something that makes her novels even more
amazing.

Mary Claire is only ten years old.

Three

Ebony

IT'S FUNNY HOW having a crush on someone makes getting dressed for school really different. When I had a crush on Jason, I noticed that I dressed up a lot more—earrings, mascara—I even used to steal a shot of my mother's Chanel No. 5 sometimes. (One time I put on so much that Barry, the drama-club coach, grabbed my arm as I walked into the auditorium and joked, "You're not supposed to *shower* in it, sweetie"—which was a really encouraging experience.)

Normally I dress kind of funky, I guess. (Well, next to Ivory's white Keds and matching cotton cardigans, it's not very difficult to come off as wacky.) Mom has all these old scarves from when she was dating Dad that I'm always stealing and putting in my hair. And I like really chunky shoes: cowboy boots, riding boots, anything with a clunky heel. Olivia calls my style "charming." When we walk down the hall, Dev calls it "deafening." So there you go.

Well, this morning I could not choose an outfit to save my life. After I got out of the shower (of course Ivory had showered and set off for school *hours* ago, practically—I swear to God, she would sleep in her locker if she could), I pretty much threw every piece of clothing I owned on my bed. Everything seemed too—I don't know, *old* Ebony, somehow.

But who was the new Ebony?

Finally I settled on a simple black A-line skirt, a blue blouse, and some plain black shoes. Very toned down for me, really, I thought, looking in the mirror. And grown-up too. Kinda. Before I left the room, I added the pair of plain gold studs that our aunt Victoria had given as matching gifts to both Ivory and me on our seventh birthday. *It's not like Charles is a job interview,* I thought, looking anxiously at the mirror. *You're not even going to see him today, I'll bet!*

Still, when I walked into homeroom, I felt weird, and I must have looked weird too. Dev, who was wearing her normal jeans and sweatshirt, raised an eyebrow. "Working on Wall Street today?" she asked, moving her knapsack off the seat next to hers so I could join her.

I put my head down on the desk immediately. "Dev, I don't know what to do," I wailed into the smooth, plastic surface—which actually felt mildly soothing.

Olivia came in just before the bell rang and slipped into the seat next to us. "What's up?" she asked urgently, taking in my crumpled pose and Dev's head shaking as Mr. Hogan, our homeroom teacher, shuffled papers around his desk and began roll call.

Dev rolled her eyes. "More boy trauma," she hissed. "Also, Ebony's becoming a corporate raider."

I jerked my head off the desk. "I don't look *that* bad, do I?" I hissed back.

Mr. Hogan raised his voice in our direction. "Ladies," he said pointedly. We quieted down.

After Mr. Hogan had gone back to taking attendance, Olivia sneaked her hand over mine. "You look very nice," she said. "Very grown-up."

Olivia is that kind of friend.

Then Dev gave me kind of a pounding on the back, which made me break into an enormous coughing fit. "Sorry," she said once it had subsided. "I was just joking, Eb. Don't worry. You'll get your man."

As we filed out into the hall for our first class, I looked around for Charles. He was nowhere to be seen.

Of course, Ms. Cabral, my Literature & Lives teacher, had yet another tome for us to tackle. Before you think I'm going to harsh on her, I have to set something straight: I really love Ms. Cabral. First of all, she always keeps a packet of Devil Dogs in her drawer, which she passes out to any students who come in and talk to her about the books after school. Second of all, she dresses really cool: even though we're just a random public high school, she's always wearing heels and exotic blouses and very beautifully colored spike heels. Third of all, she's just an awesome teacher. I space out a lot, honest. But I never space out in Ms. Cabral's class.

"Thankfully, I have convinced the administration to let me veer away from *Romeo and Juliet* this term," Ms. Cabral began. That's another really cool thing about Ms. Cabral. Other teachers either act really bored all the time or just say, "It's the curriculum," when we complain about having to do something really boring or obvious. But Ms. Cabral is always talking about "the administration" like they're evil incarnate or something.

She slapped a worn copy of some book down on my desk. I flipped it over. "In the next section we will be looking at *Twelfth Night,*" Ms. Cabral continued. "One of the most charming and unappreciated of Shakespeare's pastoral comedies."

Olivia leaned over toward me. "This is a really cool play!" she hissed. "Dev and I rented it when you were away this Christmas."

I looked at Dev. She nodded once, seriously, which meant it must have been really good. Dev's not really that big on Shakespeare—she always claims to be sick whenever Olivia and I rent *Shakespeare in Love*.

Dev leaned toward me. "Helena Bonham Carter

was in it," she whispered. I raised my eyebrows—Dev knows that H. B. C. is one of my all-time favorite actresses.

"*Twelfth Night* refers to what?" Ms. Cabral said grandly, holding up the book. That's vintage Cabral—asking us a question about the book before we even have a chance to turn to the first page.

Peter Enright—who, I suddenly realized, *knew* Charles Corey—raised his nerdy hand. "Does it refer to the twelfth night of Christmas?" he asked, his freckles flying all over the place.

I rolled my eyes, looking at the list of all of Shakespeare's comedies on the back of the book. There were over 534 correct spellings for Shakespeare, I had read somewhere in the *Guinness Book of World Records* or something. How could that be?

"Exactly!" Ms. Cabral crowed. "And in the next couple of weeks we will be discussing exactly why 'holidays' are central to this text."

I got especially anxious as I entered the lunchroom with Dev and Olivia. My stomach was fluttering like crazy—much, much more than it had ever done for Jason Warshof. *You better calm down just a little bit, Ebony,* I told myself. *Charles Corey is not going anywhere—he doesn't have an expiration date.*

Even if he *still* wasn't anywhere to be found.

I saw my sister clustered in a corner table with all the goobers from Big Think. Peter Enright was gesturing anxiously about something, and Pria Maramongolem, my sister's best friend, was gesturing angrily back at him. My sister was nodding seriously, but it was impossible to tell who she was siding with. They were probably arguing about the atomic weight of some particle or something. I craned my neck, but Charles was nowhere to be seen at their table. Shoot.

Dev bumped me from behind. "Quit dreaming," she said, pushing me toward the line while Olivia got us our favorite table and started laying out tons of little cartons filled with healthy niblets from home. (As long as I've known Olivia, I've never seen her once—once!—buy the school lunch.) "I'm *hungry*."

Dev and I both got the lovely and neon-hued grilled-cheese sandwiches with watery string beans on the side. Dev shoved two chocolate puddings on my tray without my even asking her to reach for them—she knows by now that in times of stress, I always turn to chocolate.

On the way back to our table we both couldn't keep our eyes off Ivory's corner table, though. All the kids from Big Think—and from Ivory's parties, of course—had stopped arguing and were writing quietly on small pieces of paper. While we watched, they folded them up and handed them to Ivory, who was walking around collecting them into her cardigan.

"What are they doing?" I asked Dev. I couldn't help but notice that Charles Corey still wasn't anywhere to be seen.

Dev shrugged in confusion. "It's looks like they're voting," she finally said.

We weren't the only ones with our eyes trained on the table. It's not often that one whole table in the lunchroom will go completely silent and start looking like Congress or something.

We shoved our trays in next to Olivia's brilliant display. (Some sprouty salad, marinated tofu, three oranges, and carrot sticks with peanut butter, in case you're wondering.) She was looking at the table too. "What's happening over there with your sister?" she asked.

I sighed. "Does Ivory ever tell me anything?" I asked. "I have absolutely no idea, and I really don't care." *Unless it somehow involves Charles,* I mentally added.

Actually, I had a scalp-prickling feeling that somehow it did.

As if we were communicating telepathically, Ivory began to walk toward us, clutching all the papers neatly in her sweater. I felt my throat go dry, but it wasn't me that Ivory was coming to see.

"Olivia," Ivory said when she reached us. "I need an independent auditor."

Today Ivory was wearing plain blue jeans, a blue cardigan, and a blue headband. In my head, I shook my head. "Ivory," I said. "What's going on?"

Ivory looked at me like I'd just started whistling "Dixie" in the middle of a funeral. "We're in the middle of Big Think business, okay, Eb?" she said. "I can't talk about it until all the votes are counted."

My sister is the biggest dork in the world! I screamed internally. Still, Ivory was being strangely forthcoming by even suggesting that she only couldn't talk "until the votes were counted." Did that mean she was going to tell us afterward if it had anything to do with Charles or not?

Ivory turned back to Olivia. "All the team agrees that you're a neutral party," she said. "If you could just count these ballots for us, that would be a big help."

Olivia looked at me and Dev with a poker face, then shrugged. "Sure," she said agreeably, beginning to take the ballots from Ivory. Ivory held them back for a second. "Guys, I'd appreciate it if you didn't interfere or peek at all," she said to me and Dev, looking especially hard at me.

Dev took a sip of milk. "I'll try to restrain myself," she said dryly.

I looked at my sister and nodded. I had never wanted anything in my life as much as I wanted to grab all those ballots—idiot withholding psychology works really easily on me. *I'm a neutral party too!* I wanted to scream. *Even if I'm your sister!*

But I restrained myself and tried to act like I was very fascinated with my chocolate pudding. Ivory stood slightly off to the side while Olivia patiently went through the ballots twice. "I get, um, fifteen yeses," Olivia said after a minute or so, looking up at Ivory with interest. "And one no."

Ivory's face crumpled briefly. Then she shook her head and looked like her old self again, sighing like she'd just lost her best friend. She produced a piece of paper and a pen from some pocket in her jeans and handed them both to Olivia. "Could you write down the tally?" she asked her, her voice totally flat and emotionless. "And sign it?"

Olivia leaned down to hide her face so that Ivory couldn't see her slight smile. "Sure," she answered, scribbling down something, folding the paper in half, and then signing the exposed side with a flourish.

"Can you tell us what it was all about?" Olivia asked as she handed back the paper. She turned for a second and winked at me with a big conspiratorial grin. Like I said, Olivia's a good friend.

Ivory gave a huge, rattling sigh again. "Big Think is voting," she said dramatically, "on whether to let that new guy onto the practice team."

Olivia totally kept her face blank. "Charles Corey?" she said neutrally. I felt each syllable go off in my head like a bomb.

Ivory spat out the words like each one cost her one hundred dollars. *"Charles Corey,"* she answered.

I couldn't stop myself from breaking in a little—and I had been so good up until then! "But I thought he was already on the team," I said, trying to sound like I didn't really care—I'd just had it up to *here* with Ivory's constant contradictions. "Isn't that what Mr. Rosner called to say last night?"

Ivory rolled her eyes and blew air out of the side of her mouth. *"Some* people objected to some *stranger* just dropping into the top slot without having done anything," she said, her face reddening.

Dev, Olivia, and I all exchanged looks. "Some people," Olivia murmured.

Ivory looked like she was about to go off to the gallows. "Well, thanks, Olivia," she said, gathering up all the ballots again. "See ya."

We all watched what happened next. Ivory returned to the table and murmured a few words to everyone. To the last person, the table broke out in applause. Peter Enright dashed out of the room, then returned a second later with his arm around Charles. Charles started shaking hands with everyone and sat down. When he shook hands with my sister, she looked at him like she'd like to make him eat all the ballots that were crumpled in front of her.

"Well," Dev said. "I guess we don't have to ask who voted no."

I suddenly felt a little stab of sympathy for my sister. It must be crappy to have a dream, then have someone swoop down and suddenly take it from you. Ivory had been one of the big stars on the team, but she couldn't very well keep that up with a genius on board, could she?

"Ivory works really hard at Big Think, guys," I said. "Think how she must feel."

Olivia and Dev looked at me blankly, then both cracked up. "What?" I asked.

Olivia smiled. "You just don't usually run around defending your sister, that's all," she said, her eyes crinkling with mirth.

"Yeah," Dev cracked. "Usually you seem like

you wish she went to school in a galaxy far, far away."

I put my elbows on the table. "Well, if her sworn enemy is the guy I like . . ."

"Aha!" Dev said.

". . . I don't know if that's bad or good," I finished. I refrained from looking over toward Charles's table, where Big Think still seemed to be laughing and whooping it up.

Olivia looked thoughtful. "I don't know if it's good either," she said. "I mean, if she doesn't introduce you, how are you going to get to know him? And if he's in Big Think, he might become as cliquey as the rest of that group."

"Yeah, he's going to be playing Twister down in the basement and listening to Billy Joel," I agreed miserably.

"You could join Big Think," Dev said, laughing.

I suddenly put down my soda. "Guys, I'm serious," I said, suddenly feeling triple the amount of worry I had felt the night before, when I had worried that Ivory knowing Charles already might make things—um—*awkward* for me. "I mean, auditions are next week, right? I'm going to be in rehearsals all the time. He's going to be practicing for Big Think all the time. How am I ever going to get a chance to know him?"

Olivia stroked her cheek. "Well, you could just call him," she said. "Ask him out on a date."

"Yeah," Dev agreed.

My stomach plummeted to the floor. My palms

felt icy. "Guys, first of all, that's totally terrifying," I said. Then I had another thought that was even scarier. "Also, if it doesn't work out, my sister and all of her dorky friends are going to know!" I cried. "I mean, can you imagine getting dissed practically in front of the entire nerd patrol?"

Olivia and Dev suddenly looked as freaked out as I did. "Yeah, that would totally bite," Dev agreed.

I was getting more anxious by the second, watching the back of Charles's head while he carried on some animated conversation with Pria. "I just don't want another repeat of the whole Jason Warshof incident," I said. "I mean, everyone knew I liked him. It was *so* humiliating. Then when he finally asked me out, it was like he was doing me a favor or something." My voice got a little higher. "And then when it was all over, it wasn't even worth the trouble!"

Dev looked serious. "You shouldn't feel bad about Jason Warshof," she said. "He was a total punk."

Olivia shook her head slowly. "I don't know what to tell you, Eb," she said. "Maybe your two worlds will collide somehow, and you can get to know each other."

I waved my fork around the crowded cafeteria. I hadn't even *touched* my food, I noticed. "In this zoo?" I said. "This school is so huge, people graduate next to people they barely even know."

Dev laughed. "That's true, you know," she said

to Olivia. "I mean, I've been here for three years, and I still don't know everyone in our class."

We all looked over at Charles. "Well, don't worry about it now," Olivia said, taking a sip of her water. "I mean, it's not like he's going anywhere. Anyway, you just have a bad crush. He might be awful. You really don't know anything about him."

"Yeah," Dev said. "And you've still got two more years to find out what he's like."

I didn't know what to say. On the one hand, I knew my friends were totally right. I didn't know him at all, and making this much of my feelings was ridiculous.

On the other hand, the minute I'd seen Charles's face, it was like I'd been zapped. I just *had* to get to know him—whether I liked it or not.

"I just wish there was a way I could figure out if he was likable before I did anything," I said, looking back over toward the table, where Ivory was pursing up her face like she'd just eaten sour grapes, literally. "And somehow I don't think my sister's going to be a really neutral source of information."

Dev started eating my sandwich. "A change of subject," she announced. "Did I tell you guys that I set up a meeting with Dr. Guess?"

"What for?" I asked, spooning the last of the chocolate pudding into my mouth.

Dev grinned. "Next fall," she began, "I want to play on the boys' football team."

"Dev," Olivia said, her mouth hanging open. "What are you talking about?"

Dev grinned and hid her face in her milk. "Well, you know women serve in the military right alongside men in Israel," she said after she'd swallowed. "Don't you think it's time for women to be able to QB with the boys over here?"

In drama Barry was throwing even more of a fit than usual.

I should tell you some things about Barry. (Besides the fact that he's the only teacher at Roosevelt High that anyone can call by his first name—I don't even remember his last name, to tell you the truth.) First of all, drama never used to be a big deal at Roosevelt. Proscenium, which is what our drama club is called (I know, totally unpronounceable), existed and all, but it was mostly a bunch of kids doing "Just Say No" skits about drugs and alcohol that they performed at school assemblies. There wasn't even a regular drama teacher: all the English teachers, including Ms. Cabral, used to just take the course on a rotating basis. I wasn't in high school then, but I remember sitting through some of the skits when we had to go up for all-grade assemblies, and it wasn't pretty.

All that changed when Barry came, though. First of all—he's a *real* director. He went to the Yale School of Drama, and he always knows actors on shows like *Boston Public* and *Law & Order* and *Dawson's Creek*—they're, like, his *friends*. Second of all, he directed a whole bunch of off-Broadway plays after he graduated, so it's not like he hasn't had real directing experience or like he just came into the public-school system because he couldn't make it in the real world. (He tells us all the time that his high-school drama teacher, Mrs. Blitt, was so incredible that he never wanted to do anything else but teach in high schools.) Third of all, his boyfriend, Christian, is seriously the hottest man any of us have ever seen—he's like a dead ringer for Derek Jeter. He's a lawyer, and Barry brings him to all of our performances and cast parties and stuff. At first we thought it might be a big deal to have an out gay teacher at our school, with all that Boy Scouts stuff and everything, but I guess Roosevelt High is ahead of the curve that way. In any case, Dr. Guess brought him into Roosevelt to make sure our drama program "ranked with the best in the country," and I guess he knows that no one is more perfect for that job than Barry.

Barry is short and really cute, and he always wears the same Yankees baseball cap. He's kind of skittery, though: he's always screaming at us before performances and making us all hold hands and do all these cool breathing exercises. "This is the real world, folks," is his favorite line. I think it's funny since, of course, this is actually high school. But it makes a big difference to all of us that Barry takes us so seriously.

Today Barry was even more antic than usual. "All right, people," he was shouting when I came into the room, bouncing up and down on the balls of his feet. "Settle down." He looked at me sideways. "So glad you've decided to join us, Ebony. And may I say, that is a very nice outfit."

"Thanks," I whispered, sliding into a seat next to Wallace Brooks, one of the senior boys who played Puck last year in *Midsummer-Night's Dream*. It wasn't so bad to be ragged on for coming in a little late, I guess, if you also got a compliment.

"We're having a slight change of plans, people," Barry said, holding up a book and pacing in front of the room. I couldn't read the title or anything from where I was sitting, but it looked suspiciously familiar. "I know that we were slated to do *South Pacific* for our spring play," he continued. "But orders have come from above. So instead, in conjunction with the English department, we are dropping the musical and doing *Twelfth Night*."

The room immediately erupted into groans and boos. "But Barry!" Wallace was shouting. "The spring play is *always* a musical."

Barry was holding up his hands for us to all quiet down. "People, people," he shouted. The room subsided into relative silence so Barry could talk again. "First of all, there are a few songs in every Shakespearean play," he began. Wallace began shouting again, but Barry waved his hand to silence him. "But in this play there are a million songs. You just won't be able to belt them out." Next to me, I could feel Wallace's body tensing as he tried to figure out how to object to that. "Second of all, it's synergy," Barry continued. "Both the sophomore and junior classes are reading the play, and the administration has decided that it will be fruitful to address this work through two departments. And *interesting*."

People began to babble again. "And I agree!" Barry shouted above the din.

"But *I'm* not reading the stupid book." Wallace groaned loudly.

Barry held it up and smirked. "You are now," he said. Wallace moaned as if in physical pain. I nudged him.

"Wallace, I thought you *liked* Shakespeare," I whispered. "You made such a good Puck."

Wallace looked at me with drowning eyes. "Are you kidding?" he asked. "I want a play where I can dance. And *sing!* Not march around in tights, reciting stupid verses," he spat.

I leaned back on my heels. Although I didn't want to admit it to Wallace, I had really liked the rhythms and tone of the play last year. Although big musicals were fun, Shakespeare was—*dreamy,* somehow.

"Well, you were really good," I said again. Wallace grunted.

"Now, people," Barry continued. "For the next couple of months this book is your life. You're going to read it. Love it. Live it." Then he began passing the play out to everyone who didn't have it already, hefting the stacks backward through the rows of seats. As he always did, he pointed his finger and picked a few upperclassman to start the class read through, something we always did with a new play, going around the room until everyone had played one or two parts.

"*Live* it," Barry repeated again, looking dramatically at all of us. He gave the signal for the first boy to start. "If music be the food of love . . . ," he began, twisting his T-shirt in concentration.

I didn't know yet how true Barry's words were going to turn out to be.

Four

Charles

I KNEW THIS whole Big Think thing was going to be a disaster—I just didn't know *how* big a disaster.

My first day at school was pretty cool, actually. I went to all the normal classes: history, English, health—and none of the teachers did anything weird when they introduced me. They didn't even make me stand up in the front of the room and tell the class my whole life story, which was a welcome change. By the time I got over to chemistry, I was thinking that this new school might not be so bad.

That's where my whole life of pleasant anonymity stopped, though.

"Class," said the teacher, Mr. Rosner, a sort of medium-size guy with curly brown hair and a short-sleeved shirt and brown woolen tie. (Pretty typical science-teacher attire, in my experience.) "Please welcome our new student, Charles Corey."

Mr. Rosner had me up in front of the class with him. I raised my hand in a sort of wave. A bunch of groans and halfhearted hi's floated back.

Then Mr. Rosner dropped the bomb. "Charles is something of a . . . deep thinker," Mr. Rosner said. "And we're hoping he'll be the captain of our Big Think team this year!" Then he clapped me heavily on the back like I'd just scored the winning touchdown at homecoming.

For a minute there was total silence. A few of the kids put their heads down on their desks—you could tell it was no skin off their noses either way. But more than a few looked stricken and started looking around at one another, agitation wafting off them like heat waves on asphalt. One of them, a sort of plain-looking girl with her hair yanked back in a headband, raised her hand and began to wave it around angrily. "But Mr. Rosner!" she yelled.

Mr. Rosner looked a little irritated to have his bubble burst. "Ivory," he said, gesturing toward her that it was okay to speak, even if you could tell he wished she wouldn't.

Ivory let the words out in a rush, like she'd been holding them in for two hours. "But-Mr.-Rosner-how-can-he-be-captain-when-he-hasn't-even-taken-the-test?" she rattled off like a machine gun.

Mr. Rosner looked at me slyly, then smiled, as if I'd smiled at him. (I hadn't.) I felt my stomach drop in my shoes. He was going to tell the story of my life and make me a social outcast here forever.

Again.

"Charles," Mr. Rosner began, "is something of an oddity. You don't mind me telling the class a little about you, do you, Charles?" he suddenly asked, turning to me.

It took me a minute to find my tongue. What was I supposed to say, yes? Then they'd all just think I was a mean genius too. And they'd find the truth out eventually anyway.

I was trapped.

"No," I croaked, wishing I had the guts to actually *tell* him no.

"Charles," Mr. Rosner continued, smiling at me like I was some lab rat the class had gathered around to dissect, "actually completed the typical high-school curriculum in the fourth grade."

"Du-u-u-d-e," some boy in the front row burst out, nodding energetically to his friend. Then they turned around and gave each other high fives.

"Shawn!" Mr. Rosner said sharply, and continued: "Charles's IQ is somewhere well up near 200, isn't it, Charles?" he asked, turning toward me again.

I wanted to sink through the classroom's floor into the basement, where I could curl up near the boiler and some pipes.

"Yeah," I said in a barely perceptible whisper.

"So we're very pleased to have him on the team!" Mr. Rosner said, slapping me on the back again. (Really hard.) The girl with the headband looked like she was about to explode. She raised her hand again, violently, like she wanted to thrust it through the fluorescent lights on the ceiling.

Or my head.

"But Mr. Rosner!" Ivory said. "You can't just throw all this on us at the last minute! It's not fair!"

If there's one thing I've learned from my parents, "It's not fair" is a line guaranteed to *not* get you whatever it is you want. (That's actually what my father used to say after he'd cheerfully replied, "Life's not fair!") Since teachers have to hear it all the time, I think it irritates them about a thousand times more.

Mr. Rosner was no exception. His smile turned into a thin line. "Ivory, we'll discuss this another time," he said stiffly. He gestured toward an empty desk somewhere in the third row. "Charles, why don't you take a seat, and we'll begin class for today."

In her seat Ivory gurgled and choked like a pot boiling over with spaghetti.

I sat down in the seat, my face burning. I could *feel* her staring at me, boring holes in the back of my neck.

Mr. Rosner turned and began writing on the board. "Class, please turn your textbooks to page forty-three," he said.

Suddenly a boy I hadn't even noticed before—a redhead whose entire exposed skin was completely covered with freckles, as far as I could see—leaned over. "I'm Peter," he whispered hurriedly. "We gotta talk."

I looked at him. His green eyes were friendly. "Okay," I said.

"What period do you have lunch?" he whispered. I consulted my crumpled schedule.

"Um, next," I whispered back.

Peter's face flooded with what looked like relief. "Me too," he said. "Want to have lunch with me?"

I hoped that Peter wasn't some kid who thought I would do his homework for fifty bucks. I'd met a lot—a *lot*—of kids like that before, and while the amount of money they offered you varied, the fact that they were big, slimy sleazebags never did.

"Sure," I said, trying to look as guarded as possible.

"Cool," Peter whispered. "I'll show you the good desserts."

Despite myself, I smiled. I just hoped this guy was as nice as he seemed.

In the lunchroom Peter led me over to the fastest line right away. I looked around nervously. This school was huge—the lunchroom seemed to stretch on forever, like some vast desert. "How many kids go to this school?" I asked.

"Oh, about six thousand," Peter said, not even looking vaguely impressed. "It's regional."

"Uh-huh," I said. Mom always was really serious about sending me to public schools—she'd gone to public school, and she always was railing on about how it was "the backbone of a civilized society."

If she could see all these kids throwing napkins up into the air and had to walk past the eighteen over-flowing garbage cans, though, I thought she'd probably think twice about the "civilized."

"I've been to a lot of schools," I commented as Peter steered me to a relatively quiet corner table. "But never to one this big."

Peter nodded. "How many schools have you been to?" he asked.

I thought back, mentally counting the last three or four. "Uh, twenty-six," I finally said. "I think."

Peter leaned back, looking impressed. "Is your family in the military or something?" he asked.

I smiled. Luckily I had hit on the perfect cliché a long time ago to ward off people who were too curious. "It's a really, really long story," I said, keeping my face as blank as possible so Peter wouldn't think I was secretly dying to tell it to him.

Peter nodded, his face neutral too. "Well, you'll have to tell it to me sometime," he said, thrusting one of his long, skinny arms into the air and putting it behind his head. I hoped this meant that he was ready to tell me what was going on. And if he was going to make me some stupid offer, I was going to tell him exactly where to take it.

"So, I know you're all new in school and every-thing," Peter began. "So I don't know what you know about Big Think."

I relaxed—a little. Maybe Peter was the boyfriend of the girl with the headband, and he was going to tell me to back off from the team. I flexed my nonexistent muscles and looked at my would-be opponent. I relaxed. If my muscles didn't exist yet, his clearly had never even entertained the possibility of coming into being.

"I don't know anything," I said, popping open my milk.

Peter looked relieved again. "Well, the thing is, it's a really tight club," he said. "And some of the members are pissed that Rosner's letting you in without taking the test."

Even though he was clearly giving me bad news, I didn't get the sense that Peter was one of the students who was upset. I kept my face impassive, wishing I'd never, ever heard of Big Think. If it got to be too much of a pain, I was going to drop out right away, even if it meant being tortured by my mother and Dr. Guess, with Mr. Rosner close behind. "I'll take any test," I said cagily.

Peter laughed. "Sounds like you don't have to," he said. "Listen: Mr. Rosner called me this weekend and told me everything. I don't care. I think it would be great to have you on the team."

Be careful, Charles, I told myself. *You still don't know this guy very well. And you haven't had a very good track record with people who say they'd like to have you "on the team."*

"I just wanted to give you a heads up," he said. "Ivory—that girl from class—she's probably going to make a big stink. But I figured, you just got here, right? I just wanted to tell you not to worry about it either way, if it turns into kind of a thing."

61

I took a cautious bite of my sandwich. "Uh-huh," I said, wondering what he meant exactly by "thing."

"Ivory's kind of . . . intense," Peter said. "But you shouldn't take it personally."

I swallowed. "Take what personally?" I asked.

Peter ducked his head, then looked up again. "If she acts like she wants to run you out of town on a rail," he said.

I tried to smile. I still didn't exactly get Peter's warning, but I decided to take his advice exactly: not worry too much about it. "I've been run out of town before, you know," I said hesitantly. "In fact, that's why we move so much."

Peter laughed. "Well, you definitely look like a really hard-core guy," he said.

I looked down at my white T-shirt. "You think I overdid it?" I asked.

Peter nodded. "Definitely," he said. "I heard some of the teachers are even scared to have you in their classes."

I laughed and chewed more easily. Peter was definitely an all right kind of guy. I thought. "They should be," I said, and we both burst out laughing.

From: CoreyFlakes@erols.com
To: Pebbles507@aol.com

Pebs,

So I had my first day today. You're right: this new school is really exciting

and great. I can't get over all the incredible people and the fabulous vistas
and climes.

All right—I'll stop being sarcastic.

Honestly, it's okay, I guess. I got
all sucked into this stupid thing,
though. It turns out that Big Think thing
I told you about is really more like some
exclusive country club. And there's this
one girl who's really pissed that the
coach and the teacher want to put me on
it. Like I care. I mean, I don't want to
be on it at all! But I don't want to get
into any more fights with my mom right
now. I figure if I do this, she'll lay
off, and then she won't mind if I spend
the whole summer writing.

I still haven't told my parents anything about Rush Creek. And I'm not
going to tell them until I hear from
the school. I don't want to spend my
entire life fighting with my parents.

I'm going to have to fight enough
with them if I do get in.

Keep your fingers crossed—I'm supposed to hear in the next couple of
weeks. Do you think it'll happen?
Whatever's going on, don't worry—I'll
give you all the relevant details. I'll
keep you in the loop. I know how you
love transcontinental gossip.

Just remember: if some girl named
Ivory takes a contract out on me, you
heard it here first.
   Wish you were here in a hat,
                          Charles

I was about to switch off the computer when an
instant message bleeped up on my monitor.

*Penrightman:*Charles?
*CoreyFlakes:*Who's this?
*Penrightman:*Is this Charles Corey?
*CoreyFlakes:*Who's this?
*Penrightman:*This is Peter, from school.
          This is Charles, right?
*CoreyFlakes:*How did you get my e-mail
          address?
Penrightman: Sorry to stalk you, man. Got
          it from Rosner. Just wanted
          to tell you: Ivory's going
          to try to force a vote
          tomorrow. Rosner'll probably
          let her do it. Just a
          formality, you understand.
*CoreyFlakes:*Whatever.
*Penrightman:*Listen, if you don't want
          to do it, tell me. I can
          talk to Rosner. I know it's
          stupid—you just got here,
          and now you're in the
          middle of some big thing.

```
CoreyFlakes:No, it's okay.
Penrightman:All right, dude. I'll talk
            to you tomorrow.
CoreyFlakes:Bye.
```

When I looked over the IM, I felt kind of bad. It looked like I had been really short with Peter, who seemed like a nice guy, as far as I could tell.

But I didn't know what to expect from this stupid school yet. I was in the middle of some dumb war already, it looked like.

And had only been my first day.

Well, at least they notice I'm alive here, I suddenly thought. *I never thought I would actually* wish *to be a total outcast again.*

The next day everything happened exactly like Peter had said. After chemistry Mr. Rosner called me, Peter, and Ivory in to speak with him. I could feel Ivory sitting stiffly next to me. Something told me that she wouldn't look me in the face if she were paid a million dollars to do it.

Mr. Rosner sat on the edge of a desk. "Charles, I have to apologize. It seems that I've jumped the gun." Ivory gave a little snort, and Mr. Rosner shot a steely glance in her direction.

"Some of the members of the Big Think club have objected to your automatically being admitted." I began to interject that I would do any test that they wanted me to do, but Mr. Rosner held up his hand to silence me. "Obviously you fulfill the academic requirements to become a member in good standing." Ivory snorted again, but more quietly, and Mr. Rosner was so wrapped up in his Address to the Citizens of Roosevelt High's Big Think Club that he missed it. "However, in the interests of democracy, I have concluded that it is the club members' decision whether or not they wish to add an extremely qualified candidate to their ranks." He looked at Ivory sternly. "And I can't imagine why they wouldn't, frankly."

This time Ivory didn't say or do anything. You could tell that she was just thrumming with satisfaction that she'd gotten her way.

What a pill this girl is, I thought. *I wonder what she'd think if I just told her that she could take her stupid club and—you know what with it.*

Peter broke in, and his friendly voice cut the tension. "So we're just going to take a quick vote at lunch, okay?" he asked, looking at me nervously. He leaned in and muttered, "So you can come to tonight's practice. You could come anyway, actually, if you want."

Ivory heard that one and seized up again, but then she relaxed. Clearly she knew what was going to happen and that she didn't need to push it any more to make sure I didn't usurp her rightful place on the team.

I didn't want Peter to think that I was a big baby, even though the thought of being voted out publicly actually was making me feel physically ill. *I don't mind being left out,* I thought. *But actually being voted out—by real people!—is kind of harsh.*

"So what's going to happen?" I asked, trying to make sure my voice didn't crack.

Peter was looking at me so closely that I could see the brown flecks in his green eyes. "We're all meeting at lunch," he said. "You just have to wait outside for five minutes. Then I'll come outside and tell you how it went."

I relaxed a little. I knew what Peter was really saying. If it turned out that they had voted me out, I didn't have to actually see them afterward. Peter could tell me, and I could hoof it to McDonald's or something.

For the rest of my life.

I didn't know how I'd managed to get into this mess. Nothing like this had ever happened at any of my other schools before. I also didn't know what to do about it.

I looked between Ivory and Mr. Rosner. Both of them seemed like my enemies. Peter was the only one I kind of liked, and he was over in Big Think world.

It couldn't be that bad.

"Sure," I said, wishing there was an answer like "yes" or "no," a word that when you uttered it made the whole problem go away.

I'd been out in the hall for at least fifteen minutes when Peter finally came out of the cafeteria and got me.

He'd installed me on one of those old orange,

nubbled plastic chairs that they had in every single cafeteria I'd ever seen. It must be some kind of regulation, just like those old green plastic seats with the desktops attached to them on the side.

I was doing a lot of hard thinking. Actually, a lot of hard wishing. Like, that I'd never heard of Big Think. Of Ivory whatever her name was. Of Roosevelt High.

What's it going to feel like to get voted off of a team you've never even been on? I wondered. *Nothing like* Survivor, *where at least you get to vote on who gets the million bucks at the end.*

A funny thought struck me. Perhaps if Ivory had succeeded in using her Machiavellian force to put me out of the picture, I could get Mr. Rosner to make me a proctor at Big Think or something. *That would annoy her to no end,* I thought, actually chuckling aloud at the thought of my calling, "Time!" while Ivory and her minions labored away on some problem.

Whatever happens, I thought, *you're going to Rush Creek next fall. Remember that.* And if not, I realized, wherever Dad was hired next.

Either way, you're not sticking around. This girl will be out of your hair without you having to do anything about it but wait.

That made my tensed diaphragm relax three-eighths of an inch. I knew that some guy who had lots of experience with friends and kids his own age would have found some better way to handle the situation. But I felt like I'd been tossed a paddle in a canoe on raging rapids, and I was just trying to keep afloat.

So far, I hadn't been swamped.

The cafeteria's double doors burst open. It was Peter, waving at me excitedly. "You're in!" he cried immediately.

Before Peter came by, I guess, I had been thinking mainly what I was going to do if they voted me out. I hadn't devoted any thought at all, I realized, to how I'd feel if they wanted me *in*.

I stood up, then sat down. I was feeling the last feeling I had ever expected to feel. Satisfaction— and no small amount of relief.

"That's so cool!" I said. Peter and I high-fived like I'd just done a two-handed slam into the basket.

"C'mon and meet everybody," Peter said, pushing me through the doors into the crowded lunchroom. Immediately I locked eyes with Ivory, who was sitting at a table in the corner with the rest of the Big Think people. Even from far away I could see that her brown eyes were as hard as flecks of granite.

I was in.

But what was I in *for*?

Five

Ebony

THE MINUTE I got home, I called Olivia and Dev. "Guys, you have to meet me at Stewart's," I said. "I have a plan."

Dev groaned, and Olivia gave a little laugh, like she'd heard me say that before—which she totally had. "No, seriously," I said. "It's a really good plan."

"I'm *sure* it is," Olivia said before agreeing to meet me and hanging up.

"Just don't do anything until we get there," Dev rasped.

Stewart's is the ice cream place in our town. It's been here for, like, ten thousand years. It still has all the old bar stools at the counter and marble countertop and soda machine. It also has homemade ice cream that is better than anything you could ever, ever get in the store—even Häagen-Dazs. (Believe me—I've tried.)

Also, it's the only place where I've ever, ever seen Olivia eat anything even vaguely unhealthy.

I got there first, doing my biology homework while I waited. I was so psyched about the plan, I could barely stop myself from telling it to the girl working at the counter when I ordered, and I had to force myself to look back down and study the illustration of flagella and answer the series of dopey questions that followed.

"So what's up?" Dev asked, sliding into the booth with me with her regular: coffee ice cream with hot-fudge sauce, nuts, and whipped cream. "I can assume this has something to do with the wonderful new guy in our midst?"

"Wait until Olivia gets here," I said, closing up my books and sliding them into my backpack. "But this has to do with something you guys told me this morning," I hedged.

Dev raised her eyebrows. "That I was joining the football team?" she asked. "Are you going to join it with me? That's how you're going to meet the new math genius?"

I cackled—Dev had no idea how close to the truth she really was. "Just wait," I urged.

A few minutes later Olivia rushed in, panting and out of breath. "Did I miss anything?" she asked.

"Of course not," Dev said huskily, throwing her hand out in the air across the table toward me like a circus ringmaster. "You know Ebony wouldn't begin the performance until the audience."

I fluttered my eyelashes and clapped like some old silent-movie star. Dev could seem like a real grump sometimes, but I knew she was as interested in hearing what I had to say as Olivia. "All right," I began. "Do you remember what you told me in Ms. Cabral's class this morning?"

Olivia and Dev both looked blank. "Refresh our memories," Dev finally said.

I took a deep breath. "Okay, so you've heard the deal about the spring play," I began. They both looked blank again.

"Refresh us on this one too," Olivia said, smiling.

I sighed. "It's not going to be *South Pacific*," I said. "It's going to be *Twelfth Night*."

Dev and Olivia leaned back and looked at each other. "Eb, that's nice," Olivia said, looking a little confused. "Is that part of the plan?"

"I hope you didn't drag us down here just to tell us that," Dev said, crossing her arms and looking stormy.

I made them suffer a minute more, then leaned forward like a spy sliding the briefcase filled with the enemy's plans across the table. "You guys have to promise not to think I'm stupid," I started.

"I *definitely* can't promise that," Dev interjected.

"And you have to promise to tell me whether you really think I can do it," I said, my eyes widening so that Dev would know I was serious and shut up for a second.

"Uh-oh," Dev said. "I'm getting a *baaad* feeling about this."

73

Olivia placed both hands on the table with impatience. "Eb, tell us the plan already!" she cried.

I leaned back. "Okay, remember how in *Twelfth Night,* that girl—"

"Viola," Olivia broke in. Olivia has a really uncanny memory for the names of all the characters in any book she's ever read or movie she's ever seen—even if it was years ago.

"Yeah, Viola," I said. "Remember how she dresses up as a boy to get a job with that duke guy, um—"

"Orsino," Olivia said softly.

"What was the name of the actor who played him again?" Dev asked.

"Focus," I told them both. "*Orsino.* And how at the end they fall in love and that other lady, Olivia, marries her brother?"

"Now I'm started to get a *really* bad feeling about this," Dev said. "A *Jerry Springer* kind of feeling."

I looked at Dev stonily until she stopped cracking up. "Not her own brother, you hose beast," I said. "Olivia marries *Viola's* brother, and Viola marries Count Orsino after he realizes that she's a *girl* after all."

"Eb, did you read the whole play today?" Olivia asked. "When did you learn all this?"

"We did a read through with Barry," I said dismissively. "I finished the rest during history. Anyway, the point is, *that's* what I'm going to do."

Olivia and Dev looked blank again. This was starting to stress me out. "Guys!" I said impatiently. "Are you telling me you still have no idea what I'm talking about?"

Olivia put her hands palms out on the table. "You're going to dress up as a boy?" she asked, enunciating each word like I was deaf.

Dev's face suddenly had a look of understanding. "Oh, *I* get it," she said.

"Isn't that a good idea?" I asked, beaming with relief. *Finally,* I thought.

"It's the goofiest idea I've ever heard," Dev said, hoisting a huge spoonful of ice cream and shaking it for emphasis before she shoved it in her mouth.

"Guys?" Olivia asked, looking from one of us to the other. "Will someone please tell me what's going on?"

"I mean, *you* want to put on a football uniform to do what *you* want to do," I said to Dev. "How is that so different from what I want to do?"

"Guys . . . ," Olivia wheedled.

"Well, first of all," Dev said, pausing to put at least half of her whipped-cream tower in her mouth, "I'm not going to be pretending I'm someone I'm not."

"You are if you can't *play,*" I snapped.

Olivia slapped both palms down on the table. "Guys. Someone tell me what is going on *right now.*"

Dev looked at me, then I looked at her. She shrugged and turned to Olivia. "Ebony wants to play Ivory for a day," she explained. "So she can see what Charles is like without him *knowing* she likes him."

Olivia looked at me with consternation. "Ohhh," she breathed faintly.

"And she's not allowed to do it, as far as I'm

concerned," Dev continued. "What are you going to do as Ivory that you can't do as yourself?" she asked me.

"I'm not sure," I said, getting excited just thinking about it. "It just feels like a really good idea." Dev rolled her eyes and tipped back her cup to lick the rest of her ice cream from it.

The idea had come to me like a blinding flash right at the end of class. If I just took over Ivory's life for a day or two, I realized, I could scope out Charles and see if he was a really great guy, like I thought. I could also plant some important things in his head—like, that he would probably have a lot in common with my really great sister, Ebony.

I suddenly realized that Olivia hadn't gotten anything to eat. "Olivia, you want mine?" I asked, pushing my cup of mint chocolate chip toward her.

"Yes," Olivia said, reaching with her spoon to devour it immediately. After she had eaten her first spoonful, she clapped her hands to her face. "Omigod, Eb," she said. "Remember fourth grade?"

Do I! I almost screamed aloud. "That's exactly where I got the idea," I confessed happily.

When Ivory and I were in elementary school, our school had a policy of not allowing siblings to be in the same class—I don't know why. (With Ivory and me arguing all the time, it was probably a good idea anyway.) So Ivory was in Mrs. Slavin's class, and I was in Mrs. Meek's.

Mrs. Slavin was everyone's favorite teacher. She was really pretty, with brown hair that she always wore pulled back in a high ponytail, and she smelled like whatever light perfume she wore, like wildflowers. Whenever you came to speak to her, even if you weren't her student, she always smiled at you warmly, and her eyes danced a little.

Mrs. Meek, on the other hand, was *nobody's* favorite teacher. First of all, she had been at the school for, like, twelve hundred years, even though she always looked the same—ageless. (She must have been dried out at some point, like a mummy.) Second of all, she was *really mean*. Not the kind of mean where she yelled at every student so much that eventually a parent stepped in. The kind of mean where, whenever you were near her, she wrinkled her nose like you smelled bad. The kind of mean where when you asked her a question, she always sighed and looked up like you were the most annoying kid in the world. The kind of mean where, if you got a bad grade on a test, she would wave it around and tell the whole class how low you'd scored before she slapped it faceup on your desk.

And remember, this was just *fourth grade*.

Well, I was really, really jealous of Ivory's luck in getting Mrs. Slavin, of course. And by Christmas, I was so miserable in Mrs. Meek's class that I would have done almost anything to get into Mrs. Slavin's.

I guess I did kind of a bad thing. I started coming home and talking about how great Mrs. Meek's class was. About how we got to do really fun projects all the time. About how Mrs. Meek had totally changed and was really the best teacher in fourth grade that year, hands down.

(Why didn't I just tell my parents how much I hated the class, you ask? Well, I don't know. I guess I didn't because I knew that unless I could show them how Mrs. Meek was really a very bad person, they would just tell me to put my chin up and learn from it. That's what you get from ex-hippie parents—they think everyone is secretly good inside, even your heinous, lizardlike teacher. Which is *so* not true.)

Anyway, it all blew up in my face. After promising to do the dishes for a week, I got Ivory to agree to switch places with me for one day. (I think I had a fantasy that Mrs. Slavin would recognize my true self, then like me so much that she would insist that I switch into her class too. That's the kind of thing you think in the fourth grade.) I spent a heavenly day in Mrs. Slavin's class, learning my times tables and making a Thanksgiving diorama. And then when I got home, there was Ivory, in tears, screeching to my parents about how mean Mrs. Meek was and how she hadn't let Ivory go to the bathroom for a full *hour* after she had asked.

Well, it didn't turn out all that badly, even if my parents had a total hissy fit—both over what I had done and what Mrs. Meek had done. Mrs. Meek ended up taking an early retirement after some meeting with my parents where she called me a "dishonest little sneak" in front of the principal. But I was totally grounded for a *month,* both for "not being honest with us" and "putting your sister in such a bad situation."

We had a really good substitute, Mr. Huey, for the rest of the year. Actually, he became even *more* popular than Mrs. Slavin.

"I remember," I said to Olivia. "We got Mr. Huey!"

Olivia shook her head. "But Eb, that was *fourth grade,*" she said worriedly.

Dev shook her head too. "Eb, what are you going to do when Mr. Rosner asks you a *real* science question?" she asked. "Find Ivory somewhere, ask her the answer, then run back?"

I reached over and took the last spoonful of the mint chocolate chip. "It's just for a day or two," I said.

"What about Pria?" Dev asked. "You'll have to tell her."

I groaned and slapped myself. "I forgot about that," I said. "But it's a minor glitch."

"Ivory will *never* agree to it," Olivia said.

I was thinking about Pria. "Pria can keep a secret," I decided.

"Are you going to go to Big Think practice and everything?" Dev asked, shaking her head. "What are they going to think when you suddenly don't know anything?"

"I'll do what Barry taught me," I said, suddenly feeling the confidence of ten Ebonys. "I'll improvise."

Olivia and Dev looked at each other, and they *both* groaned. I licked the spoon and tried to ignore them.

★   ★   ★

By the time I walked home, however, I was feeling a little more trepidation. After all, Ivory was going to want to know why I wanted to switch places with her, wasn't she? I ran through a couple of scenarios in my mind while I waited for her to get home from her regular Big Think Tuesday practice.

Ebony Gets Ivory to Switch,
Act 1, Scene 1

EBONY: Ivory, I've got to ask a big favor.

IVORY: [*turning from computer*] No.

EBONY: [*trying to block screen with hands*] Just listen a sec.

IVORY: Eb, whatever it is, the answer is no.

EBONY: Iv [*pronounced I've*], it's a teensy, weensy little favor.

IVORY: Well, this is a big old fat no.

Ebony Gets Ivory to Switch,
Act 1, Scene 1, Take 1

EBONY: Iv, can I talk to you for a sec?

IVORY: [*turning and peering over tops of glasses*] What?

EBONY: Remember that thing we did in fourth grade?

IVORY: [*turns around back to screen, refuses to speak to* EBONY *for the rest of the evening*]

Ebony Gets Ivory to Switch,
Act 1, Scene 1, Take 2

IVORY: Ebony, what are you doing?
EBONY: [*skulking around bedroom door*]
Nothing.
IVORY: Then why are you skulking around
my bedroom door?
EBONY: Because I have to ask you a really big favor.
IVORY: [*slams door in* EBONY's *face*]
EBONY: [*falls to knees, pounds force-
fully on wood*] Ivory, I need you to
switch places with me so I can get to
know Charles Corey in a normal, every-
day kind of way without him suspecting
he's falling in love with me all along!
IVORY: [*silence*]

When it actually came down to it, though, asking Ivory for the favor was strangely easy. I was up
in my room, finishing up my homework, when I
heard her come in. Mom and Dad weren't even
home yet. She walked up the steps and went into
her room. I tiptoed across the hallway and knocked
on her closed door.

Ebony Gets Ivory to Switch for Real,
Act 1, Scene 1
IVORY: [*dully*] Yeah?
EBONY: [*forced cheer*] Iv? Could I come

talk to you for a sec?

IVORY: [*groans, bedsprings turning*] Okay. Just a minute. [*Answers door, blinking*] What?

EBONY: Can I come in for a sec?

IVORY: [*turns, leaves door ajar*] I guess. [*Flops on bed, facedown*]

EBONY: [*more forced cheer*] Iv, I need a little favor.

IVORY: [*silence*]

EBONY: I need you to do something really silly.

IVORY: [*silence*]

EBONY: [*pause*] I need you to switch places with me for a little bit.

IVORY: [*silence*]

EBONY: [*urgently*] I can't tell you why, though. But I'm willing to discuss any and all payback options.

IVORY: [*grinds head into pillow*]

EBONY: [*fearful pause*] Iv? It won't be like fourth grade. I promise.

IVORY: [*unintelligible*]

EBONY: What?

IVORY: [*unintelligible*]

EBONY: [*cups ear*] What?

IVORY: [*with irritation*] I said, I guess I wouldn't mind being someone else for a day or two right now.

So that was that.

Six

Charles

GET THIS: THE first meeting with the Big Think club was actually kind of *fun*.

I don't want to go overboard. It's not like it was a midnight cruise in the Caribbean or anything. Or meeting Quentin Tarantino. I mean, that would be *really* cool.

Still, it wasn't half bad. We all met in this room in the basement of the school, in the big room where the band practices during the day. There were all these chairs and stands stacked up against three of the walls. The old grand piano in the corner had its case shut down with a huge combination lock.

"So I guess I can't do my nightclub-singer act?" I muttered to Peter, jerking my head toward the piano.

Peter looked thoughtful. "If we can't crack a stupid lock, we're probably not much of a team, right?" he mused. "Still, I bet having the football team do it would be faster," he added, making me crack up.

The meeting started off with a bunch of pizzas and sodas. While we were chowing down, most of the team members came over to meet me and introduce themselves. A lot of them apologized for the voting thing, saying things like, "It wasn't really my idea, man," and, "I hope you didn't mind that stupid voting thing that Ivory made us do." The whole time Ivory sat in the corner with her friend, a tall Indian girl with long, dark hair, whom I had gathered was named Pria. The whole day hadn't reduced the force of Ivory's laserlike glare.

After a girl named Lindsay had wandered over to talk to some other friends, Peter leaned toward me. "Ivory'll thaw once we get started," he said. "You'll see."

As it was, I didn't care if Ivory remained encased in a block of ice for the next six million years. "I'll believe it when I see it," I said, swigging a root beer like a guy in some beer ad. All those people coming over to meet me had given me a strange, happy prickle in the back of my scalp. It was probably more people than I'd ever talked to at all my old schools put together. And instead of making me want to sink through the floor with embarrassment, being the most popular guy in the room was actually making me feel like what all those people on late night informercials called "a people person."

"All right, Thinkers," Mr. Rosner finally said. "Let's get started."

The first part of the practice was pretty standard—a lot like the math meets I'd sometimes attended at my other schools when I was dragged in by the principal or the coach, just like here. We pulled out two long tables and sat across from each other while Mr. Rosner passed out a series of xeroxes. Each one had a different problem: logic, calculus, probability, trigonometry, whatever. Mr. Rosner stood in front of the two tables with a stopwatch. The first person to solve the problem correctly got a point for it. The team that had the most points at the end of ten problems won the game. Individual high scorers also got ranked on a big board that Mr. Rosner had pulled out from the corner. Looking it over, I saw that Ivory was one of the top scorers in almost every category.

Including math.

"And . . . begin," Mr. Rosner said, once we'd all gotten the first problem in front of us and Pria, Ivory's tall friend, had distributed her bundle of tiny yellow pencils.

Looking down at the problem, I recognized it as a certain type I'd worked on a lot in second grade. I was about to lean over and attack it when I stopped myself.

Charles, why don't you just relax? I thought. *You don't need to decimate everyone this second. Why don't you see how the other people do before you go in with both barrels firing? They seem to like you now, but they might change their minds if they think you're just out to make them feel stupid.*

After a couple of minutes and a lot of pencil scratching, there was a shout from the other table. "Finished!" a girl cried.

Mr. Rosner clicked the stopwatch and looked expectant. "Answer?" he said.

The voice rose up triumphantly. "Forty-seven thousand miles," the girl said.

"Correct," said Mr. Rosner, leaning down to make a notation on the chart.

It was Ivory, of course.

It went on that way for the next half hour or so. Ivory didn't finish all the problems first—she missed all the ones that required a lot of trig, I noticed—but she got a lot of them just the same. By the last problem our table had one point, her table eight.

"Flying under the radar?" Peter whispered to me.

"Something like that," I whispered back.

Mr. Rosner looked sternly in our direction. You could tell that he was just beside himself that I hadn't answered every question. In fact, I hadn't answered any.

Well, take that, I thought, feeling that I was getting revenge on every teacher who had ever assigned me extra proofs "for fun" or made me sit and discuss various theorems with them after school for hours. *I just promised to show up, not to be Mr. Terminator Genius Head.*

"And . . . begin," Mr. Rosner said as the last question was passed around.

I looked down. This was a really old problem that I'd seen a million times—in fact, it seemed really easy compared to all the problems we'd been doing so far. It went like this: "You have nine coins. One of them is false and is lighter than the others. You have a scale that will remain correct for only two attempts at weighing. If you can't find the false coin for the king, he will cut off your head. How do you find the false coin?"

I twirled my little pencil for a second as if I was going to write something down, than gave in to myself. I raised my hand.

"Charles!" Mr. Rosner said, sounding especially hearty and relieved.

"You split any six coins into three and three," I said, trying to sound like I'd thought about it for a while. "If they are equal, you turn to the last group of three and weigh any two. You either find the lighter coin immediately, or it's the one you've left out. If the first two sets are unequal, you weigh the lighter set the same way—taking two and leaving one out. Then you can keep the fake coin—and your head."

"Correct!" Mr. Rosner called, practically before I had even finished talking.

"A-*ha*," Peter said.

Mr. Rosner looked down at his chart again. "That makes team two the winner, with a total of eight to team one's two," he said. "Ivory, you are

87

the high scorer, with five points," he said, looking in my direction instead of Ivory's. He licked his lips, then clearly decided to go ahead and speak the obvious. "Now, Charles, don't be shy," he urged. "Don't be afraid to jump in."

The rest of the team murmured friendly assent.

I was looking down at the tabletop, twirling the soft tip of my pencil into the palm of my hand. I didn't need to look up to know that despite her high score, Ivory was glowering at me like my mom used to when I'd just tracked mud in all over her nice clean floor.

As usual.

When the meeting was over, Peter and I walked out together. "Which way are you headed?" he asked.

I still hadn't gotten exactly used to where everything went in the town. "Um . . . this way, I think," I said, pointing to the left. Being a so-called genius unfortunately hadn't given me anything resembling a sense of direction.

"That's my way," Peter said. We started walking down the sidewalk. Blossoms had just come out on all the trees, and the air smelled really beautiful. That was one thing nice about moving back to the East Coast, I realized. The four seasons, instead of the relentless sunshine of California.

"That was really cool, how you knew all the answers to all of those history questions," I offered, not just trying to make conversation, but really meaning it. I had been amazed at how much

Peter knew once we got past the math and science sections.

After the math part of the practice, the teams had split up again into even smaller teams, and Mr. Rosner had fired a battery of questions at us in the basic Trivial Pursuit categories: literature, science, geography, and history. Peter had scored really well on all of them, but he had completely blown everyone else away with dates, times, and names in history.

For my part, it was nice to really *not* know the answers to some things for once. I mean, I definitely knew a lot of them. (That's the annoying thing about having a photographic memory—if you've ever read something once, it just blinks up whenever you need it, like a Web page.) Still, there was plenty of stuff that I didn't know.

"The female heroine of Thomas Hardy's *The Return of the Native* . . . ?"

"The year the Sino-Japanese war commenced . . . ?"

"The sibling duo who composed and wrote the text to the Negro National Anthem . . . ?"

"The author of the comic strip *Maus* . . . ?"

"The composer of *Afternoon of a Faun* . . . ?"

"Yeah," Peter said. "My grandmother's really into history books, I guess. She leaves so many biographies and autobiographies around the house, I got used to reading them myself." He chuckled. "I also watch a lot of A&E," he admitted.

I looked over at him. Peter wasn't that tall, but he was so skinny that he looked a lot taller than he was. Actually, he looked kind of like a young, white, redheaded version of my dad.

"That's how I got into movies," I ventured, hoping that I wasn't getting too personal for what was basically our first real conversation. "My mom's always watching them."

Peter looked up at me like he had been chewing on something a little. "Want to come over for dinner?" he asked suddenly. "My grandmother's a really good cook."

I felt the funny scalp prickle again. Of course, I had gone for dinner at Mary Claire's house a bunch of times. But that was mostly because we would be hanging out in the backyard when her dad called us in for spaghetti or goulash or whatever. This was, I realized, the first time another kid had *invited me to his house*.

"Sure," I said.

Peter's house wasn't very far from the school. It was small and painted brown, at the end of a little side street. The porch was covered with wisteria and all sorts of hanging plants. "This is the palace," Peter said, opening the screen door and ushering me over the threshold.

Inside, it was cool and dark. Right away I noticed the difference between the furniture in his house and mine. Since we're always moving so much, all of our stuff is constantly in boxes, which surround whatever couch my mother's just ordered from the Door Store or IKEA. But Peter's house was filled with what were clearly antiques—heavy wooden furniture, Persian carpets—things that looked like they'd stayed in the same place for centuries. Also, the air smelled like the air outside—was that potpourri?

"Penny?" Peter called up the steps. "Penny, are you home?"

I looked toward the kitchen. I didn't see anyone grandmotherly totter out. "Who's Penny?" I finally whispered to Peter, wondering if it was a dog or something.

Peter looked at me strangely. "My *grandmother*," he said. "She's probably doing yoga or tai chi—she meditates a lot."

"Oh," I replied with surprise. I didn't know any grandmothers that you could call by their first names. Both my grandfathers had died before I was born. My dad's mother was down in Florida, living in one of those really cushy senior communities like Jerry's parents on *Seinfeld,* with senior buffets and ballroom dancing and visiting comedians. My mom's mother came out to visit us once or twice every year. She was a plump, smushy woman who smelled like Dove soap and always seemed to think I was still eleven.

"Your grandma does yoga?" I asked, like my brain moved at the speed of molasses.

Peter waved me into the kitchen and took two V8s out of the fridge. "Sorry there's no soda," he said. "Penny's a health nut." He ripped the plastic top off his and gulped it in a few swallows, then grabbed a chair. We sat down at the fifties-style

91

kitchen table. "She was a dancer, actually, when she was younger."

"A, um, ballet dancer?" I asked. I was just hoping it wasn't an "exotic" cancan dancer—that might be too much to wrap my head around, even if I'd just seen *Moulin Rouge* a few weeks ago.

Peter shook his head. "My grandmother studied with that dancer, you know, Twyla Tharp?" he asked, tossing his can into the corner garbage.

I shook my head. I had never heard of her.

"The founder of modern dance!" Peter said. "Man, you suck on the history stuff."

I laughed. "I know," I said. "All I know is music stuff because of my mom."

Peter cocked his head. "What's the deal with your parents again?" he said. "What do they do, I mean?"

I ducked my head and fiddled with my can of V8. I didn't want to have to tell him all about my weird family—he might regret trying to become my friend when he heard how we lived on Chinese takeout and that my mother sometimes got up in the middle of the night and started banging out some sonata. Not to mention the constant moving around. I looked up. "What about yours?" I asked.

Pete nodded seriously, like he understood how uncomfortable I was without my saying anything. "They were actually killed in a car accident," he said. "When I was three."

I suddenly felt like a three-mile-wide foot was sticking out of my mouth. I was genuinely shocked—and I didn't know what to say. All I could do was let my mouth hang open for a minute.

"Don't worry," Peter said, smiling a little. "Everyone asks that question if I forget to tell them first."

"Wow, man, I'm really sorry," I finally managed, then mentally smacked myself on the forehead. If Peter wanted sympathy, he'd ask for it, right? People must always be shaking their heads at him and making comforting little moues.

Luckily we were interrupted before I could say anything else stupid. A birdlike, buzzing vision floated into the room. It had short, spiky hair so black, it was almost blue, bright green eyes, and at least five turquoise necklaces draped around its neck. It was dressed in red warm-up pants and an Indian-print top. "Well, what do we have here?" it cackled, looking at me with amusement.

It was Penny.

Peter laughed. "Penny, meet Charles Corey," he said. "This is the guy I told you about." He turned to me. "You can call her Penny," he confided. "Everyone does."

Penny shot Peter a hawklike glare and strode over to the counter, where there was a bowl of oranges. She began to peel one with an ornate little knife. "Now, remember, young man," she said to Peter, pointing the knife at him momentarily. "I'm not so old that I can't tell a young man to call me by my first name all by myself. In fact, you may find yourself calling me Grandmother Enright if you're not careful."

Peter cracked up. "Yeah, speaking up for yourself is really hard for you, I've noticed," he said.

Penny walked over and ruffled his hair affectionately. "What time is it?" she suddenly asked, looking around like she'd just lost a kid in a department store. I jerked my wrist to look at my watch, but she had already moved on. "Are you boys ready to help me make dinner?" she asked imperiously, the wrinkles around her eyes crinkling into a smile as she looked from Peter to me.

Apparently we were.

To: Pebbles507@aol.com
From: CoreyFlakes@erols.com

Hey, Pebs—
You know how much I hate to admit that you're right.

Okay, remember that dumb Big Think thing I was all messed up with? Well, it actually turned out okay. That girl Ivory made the whole group vote on whether or not I could be in it. (Remember how much I was shaking in my boots about that one?) But get this—the whole group (except her, of course) voted yes.

I didn't think I'd care, but I kind of did.

The group itself is kind of fun—I mean, it's just like a game show for

kids or something. We get pizza at
practice. And I guess I wouldn't mind
getting some money for college—even if
I've already kind of gone to college.

I could use it in film school, right?

Oops, I actually just thought of
that. That's true. That would solve the
problem of my parents being freaked out
if that's what I want to do anyway.

Anyway, the really cool thing is this
guy Peter Enright. He's a sophomore
here, and he knows any date and time of
anything that has ever happened in the
history of the world, I swear. He totally tore up the history section. It
was really impressive.

I just got back from dinner at his
house, actually. He lives with his
grandmother, Penny, because his parents
both died in a car accident when he was
three. Isn't that awful? It made me
feel like a jerk for always complaining
so much about my parents. I mean, at
least I have parents.

Penny is really cool, though. She's
like seven hundred and eighty years
old, but you can't really tell. She
does yoga! We both helped her make
dinner. I have no idea what it was. We
must have cut up something like a
thousand vegetables, and then she

hauled out some kind of noodles and stir-fried the whole thing with this enormous tin of spices that she said she got in India in 1967. I'm not kidding.

Also, here's the really cool thing. I told Peter about all the movies we used to do. Penny said she'd be interested in seeing them—even in acting in some! She said she has plenty of hats. Plus a grandson to do the male roles.

Don't worry that I'm trying to replace you. Of course, no one will ever equal your thespian genius—that's a given.

Have you finished your latest? What was it—a novel that's written entirely backward, right? You better send it soon. By attachment, though, 'cause my printer's broken.

Say it, don't spray it,

Charles

Seven

Ebony

IVORY AND I spent all of Wednesday afternoon practicing for the next day's switch.

We were standing in the middle of my room, with half of Ivory's clothes joining mine on my bed, which was its usual disaster area.

"Is this really how you want me to do my hair?" Ivory was asking.

I had decked her out in one of my favorite outfits—a blue-and-red-patterned wraparound skirt, a white blouse, and a jean jacket. Ivory had refused to put my boots on yet, and I was struggling to pull her hair back into its normal, curly state from the resolutely straight style she favored with a glass of water and a comb.

"Ow!" Ivory said, leaning around to glare at me.

"Sorry," I said.

Ivory snatched the comb and water from me.

97

"Let me do it. You're going to rip half the hair off my head."

I flopped down on the bed, unable to believe that Ivory and I had been born with the same hair. While I'd been using leave-in conditioners and wearing mine curly for years, Ivory always took a blow-dryer and a straightening comb to hers every time she washed it, a process I was not looking forward to tomorrow morning.

I watched Ivory pull the wet comb through her black hair, making the strands slowly crinkle into curls. I'd scarcely had the nerve to ask why Ivory was being so agreeable about this whole switcheroo thing. Even though I was dying to find out, I was also much too incredibly relieved that she didn't seem to have an ounce of curiosity about *my* reasons to worry that much about *hers*.

"There," Ivory said, standing back from the mirror to get a better look at herself. "That's your mop head, all right."

I threw a T-shirt at the back of her head. "You're going to have to do a little makeup," I said. "To match the mop head."

Ivory shrugged, which was weird. I'd been worried about getting her into my normal face since Ivory had always *hated* makeup, claiming that it made her feel like her skin was covered with "tiny crawling ant babies." I scrambled over to get my makeup box and quickly put on a little mascara and lip gloss before she could change her mind.

I had just swept on some navy mascara when

there was a knock at the door. "Girls?" my mom said.

Ivory and I looked at each other—me in panic, her in irritation. "Just—just a second!" I finally stammered.

Mom knocked again. "What are you doing in there?" she asked.

Ivory finally took over. "Mom, we are fifteen years old!" she said. "Can we please just be allowed to have a private conversation without the KGB coming in?"

There was silence on the other side of the door. "All right," Mom's voice called out. There was something weird about it. I decided what it was after a moment. It was nutty because she sounded *pleased*.

Ivory was shaking her head. "Mom is *totally* out of control," she muttered, putting the comb back on my bureau.

I suddenly realized how long it had been since Ivory had talked about Mom and Dad. Or about school. Or about *anything*.

I put my hands on my hips. I was wearing Ivory's normal jeans-and-cardigan ensemble, with a bandanna wrapped around my head for practice. I also had on Ivory's glasses, which weren't perfect but were close enough to my own contacts prescription that I could stand it for a day or two.

"Hey, Ivory, is everything all right?" I asked. Ivory was leaning in close to the mirror, examining some nonexistent blemish on her chin. "I mean, with school and everything?"

Ivory turned around to peer at me. She hadn't put her own contacts in yet—she hated contacts; they made her blink four times more, she claimed—and I knew I was just a big fuzz ball to her. "What do you mean?" she asked warily.

I came a little closer so that I would come into focus. Our two schedules were lying on the floor near her feet—hers neat and sharp as if it had just come out of the envelope, mine totally crumpled and half ripped off the ditto backing. "I just meant, we haven't talked in a while," I said lamely.

Ivory turned around completely and faced me. Even though when you're a twin, you get used to the weirdness of having someone around that looks so much like you, Ivory and I had looked so different for so long that seeing Ivory dressed exactly like me—in my *actual* clothes—was still a little startling. I made a quick mental note to remember that my black boots really, really didn't go well with that skirt.

Ivory turned back to the mirror. "I'm doing well enough that I want to switch lives with you for a little while," she said. "Does that answer your question?"

Her answer hit me like a quick punch in the stomach. I swallowed. Ivory was my sister, after all. Even though she annoyed me to no end, that didn't mean I didn't care about how things were going with her.

Even though I hadn't been acting like it lately.

I took a step closer to her and put my hand on

her arm. "Um, do you want to talk about it?" I asked.

But Ivory shook off my arm and picked up the lip gloss again. She wasn't the Headband Queen of Roosevelt High anymore, but she was still definitely the Secrets Queen of our house.

"Show me how to use this, will you?" she asked, removing the wand from the sparkly little container. "If I'm going to be you for a day, I don't want to look like I put on my makeup with a rake."

I smiled.

"You have your reputation to keep up, after all." Ivory hummed, gliding the wand over her lips like she'd been doing it for years. She popped the wand back into the container and turned around to face me. "Good?" she asked. I crossed my arms and scrutinized her from head to toe.

"Hey," I said with surprise. "We could almost be twins!"

My first day as Ivory started off with a piercing alarm ringing at least forty-five minutes before I ever normally got out of bed.

"Aaaaahhh!" I said, leaning over to switch it off. I had set it so early to make sure that I was still going to have time to straighten my hair. In the cold light of day, my plan was beginning to fill me with the first curdlings of panic. A hot shower would cure it, I decided, grabbing my robe and staggering into the bathroom.

As I rinsed the last suds of Ivory's shampoo from

my hair, I was suddenly seized by another worry. What if *Ivory* hadn't been able to go through with the plan?

As the last water trickled into the drain, I knew that wasn't my problem. When Ivory said she would do something, she did it. I was the one who got all tangled up in knots and tried to wiggle out of responsibilities.

I sighed and plugged in the hair dryer.

The night before, I had called Olivia and Dev to warn them that the plan was going off. Olivia groaned like a deep-sea monster was oozing out of her chest, and Dev actually began speaking to me in *Hebrew*.

"Dev, Dev," I yelled to her, laughing. "Speaking to me in a language I don't understand is not going to make your argument any stronger."

Dev stopped rattling off hysterically for a sec. When she spoke again, her voice—in English—sounded worried. "I just think this could be *really* bad," she said. "Like even a thousand times worse than Jason Warshof."

I laughed, although butterflies were brewing in my stomach too, as much as I tried to quiet the flapping of their wings. "Don't worry!" I said. "They do this in the movies all the time."

"They jump off hundred-story buildings too," Dev warned me. "And they use stuntmen. Don't forget that part."

As I rubbed cream through my hair and pressed it through the stream of hot air behind the plastic comb, I was trying to forget the image of plummeting to the sidewalk as best as I could, where *g* equaled something that only Ivory would be able to figure out. *Hey, Ebony,* I told myself, trying to give me the pep talk my best friends weren't handing out. *Just think of this as your first major starring role.*

Don't worry about the fact that you're not in a play.

I had arranged to meet Pria outside the school at eight o'clock since she and Ivory had the exact same schedule. (They'd been doing that on purpose since seventh grade.) I ran up, huffing and puffing, at eight-oh-five.

Pria almost gasped when she saw me. "Ebony?" she whispered.

"Yeah!" I answered, brushing back a few of the strands that had strayed out of the teeth of Ivory's favorite pink headband in my mad rush to get there on time. The straightening had worked out much better than I could have hoped—only a little puffier than Ivory's normal sleek look—but it had left me with a massive arm ache and a crick in my neck.

Pria shook her head. "I mean, I always knew you guys were twins, but this is . . ."

"Really amazing," I said, catching a glimpse of myself—or my sister—in the wavy glass of the school's door.

Pria giggled and shook her head again. "You guys are crazy," she said.

As we walked through the front doors together, Pria gave me a funny, sideways look. "Can I ask you something?" she said. "Why are you guys doing this? Ivory won't tell me *anything*."

Strangely glad to hear that Ivory was as close mouthed with her best friend as she was with her sister, I clutched my—Ivory's—books closer to my chest. "Sorry," I said breezily, looking around for Ivory and Dev and Olivia, who were nowhere to be seen. *They must be off making awkward conversation in homeroom,* I thought, wishing I could just peek in and see how everything was going in "my" life for a second.

The first bell of the day clanged. "Let's get to homeroom," Pria said. "Ivory's *never* late, believe me."

The first couple of periods of the day were all pretty uneventful. Mostly I handed in the home-work Ivory had given me the night before and tried to stay quiet. (There was one tense moment in French—I took Spanish, of course—when Madame Galinsky rattled off some extremely long question at me, but when I tried to look like I was thinking deeply about it and answered, "*Non,* Madame," I went mercifully undetected since that just so happened to be the right answer.)

I knew that Charles and Ivory had chemistry together, so before the bell rang, Pria and I ducked into the bathroom so I could fix anything that was awry. (It wasn't like I could put on extra lipstick or anything—but I could try to put Ivory's best face forward.) I looked at myself in the mirror. I looked exactly like Ivory had looked for the past five years.

"You're good," Pria said, glancing at me before

leaning over to wash her hands. "Ivory all the way."

I looked at Pria with new admiration. I'd always thought she was kind of a drag—just Ivory's silent, boring, badly dressed friend, exactly the kind of girl who still wore bunny-feet pajamas at Ivory's sleepovers. But in fact, all day she'd been really funny—cracking jokes about classmates and telling me funny tics of Ivory's that I didn't even know about (like how Ivory liked to rip all the edges off notebook paper before she handed in homework—even if it was Pria's homework). And besides that, she'd been really *nice* to me and helped me out, when all I'd ever done for her was to give her a sullen "hey" from time to time.

"Um, Pria," I said as she flicked the water from her fingertips and put them under the dryer. "I just wanted to tell you: thanks for helping me out so much today."

Pria looked over at me and smiled. "Are you kidding?" she said. "This is the most exciting thing that's happened at school since Timmy Marx rode his mountain bike through the entire building until Dr. Guess ran him down with a lacrosse stick."

We both cracked up.

I walked into Mr. Rosner's classroom behind Pria so that she would guide us to our "regular" seats. It was funny to see how, while Dev, Olivia, and I always sat toward the back, in the middle, Pria and Ivory were seemingly always locked into the front right-hand corner.

I couldn't help but notice that Charles and Peter

were sitting really close to us—just four seats away from me and Pria, in fact.

Pria leaned over to whisper to me. "Now, Ivory's usually really talkative in class," she said. "But just look like you're still mad over the Big Think thing, and maybe Ros will back off."

I had a thought. I had known Ivory was pissed about Charles being let on the team. But could that explain the *whole* reason that she was so upset at home?

I made a mental note to really try to find out what was going on.

Maybe Pria knew more than she thought she did. I looked at her with questioning eyes.

"Does that have anything to do with what you guys are doing?" Pria asked, totally oblivious to my poor maneuvers and still trying to get the goods on me and Ivory.

I raised my eyebrows and shrugged, trying to look mysterious and poker faced at the same time. It sort of gave me a headache. It was time to get in character for "Ivory" anyway, even if I'd barely cracked the textbook this semester.

"All right, class," Mr. Rosner said, snapping a piece of chalk immediately and leaning down to pick it up. "We're going to do some labs today. Go to your stations."

I shot Pria a panicked look. "Don't worry," she whispered. "You're my lab partner."

"Ivory," Mr. Rosner said, making me jump—I was so worried that I wasn't going to answer to

Ivory's name that I almost had a heart attack any-time anyone said it. "Why don't you go with Charles today since he's new? Pria, you go in with Linda and Mark."

I had received an unexpected stroke of luck, but I didn't know if it was good or bad. Panic surged in my throat. I knew Ivory was pissed at Charles for stealing the genius chair from her. Mr. Rosner must have arranged this "exercise" just to give the two a chance to bond.

Either way, whether I liked it or not, it was "I" who was going to be doing the bonding—big time.

Even though this was what I had been wishing for all day, I was scared to look Charles in the eye. So I shuffled through Ivory's stuff for her lab note-book. After going through her stuff three times, though, I had to admit that it wasn't there.

I raised my hand. "Mr. Rosner," I said, trying to sound as much like my sister as possible. "I forgot my lab notebook."

I swear to God, the entire class became silent. Could this really be such an event? I—Ebony—for-got my lab notebook every other day.

"You're taking after your sister!" Mr. Rosner said after recovering from the shock. He reached into his drawer and drew out two new notebooks. "Why don't you take this one for today, Ivory? Charles, this one's yours."

Charles and I walked over to the last empty lab table like we were walking to the altar. I had to stop myself from shaking a little at being so close to him.

As we put our books down, without thinking I gave him a hesitant smile.

Ebony, remember! Ivory hates *Charles!* I scolded myself.

But Charles seemed to take Ivory's new friendliness as some kind of signal. Flipping the xeroxed lab over to the first page, he smiled back. "You did really well at practice the other day," he offered hesitantly.

Why, he *was* a really nice guy, I thought, looking at his eager smile. Shy, even. That threw the arrogant, evil genius Ivory seemed to be afraid of straight out the window.

"Thanks," I said, looking down at my notebook so he wouldn't see my blush.

Charles cleared his throat, and started assembling various vials and . . . pipettes, or whatever they were called. "Can you pass me the retort?" he asked.

My heart jumped into my throat. The only retorts I knew about were the ones my mother flung back at my father in their occasional fights. I looked over the black surface of the lab table and tried to look confused. "Um . . . I don't see it," I finally said.

Charles gave me a funny look, then leaned past me. He smelled soapy, like detergent and some piney men's deodorant. It was a *big* improvement over the sweaty funk some of the unwashed masses of our school seemed to favor.

"It was right in front of you," he said, holding a

funny-shaped tube up to his face. "Wait . . . are you still testing me or something?"

I gave him a nervous laugh. What was he talking about? Ivory must have been quizzing him every other second or something to try to put him in his place.

Charles smiled. "Well, I had to take chemistry too," he said.

Thank God, I thought. If he had only been a math genius, we would have handed in the scrappiest-looking lab Mr. Rosner had ever seen.

"You know," Charles said as he began to stick various powders into a test tube, checking back with the assignment every couple of seconds, "I just wanted to apologize about the Big Think thing. Honestly, if I had known it was such a problem for you . . . your members," he said, looking at me over the tops of his glasses, "I would have told Dr. Guess no right away."

Boy, is he lucky I'm not Ivory, I thought. *She would have taken this Bunsen burner and cracked him right over the head.* Ivory *hated* any hint of pity or condescension from anyone, even if that someone was only trying to be polite.

Luckily I wasn't Ivory. "That's okay," I said. "I'm really happy to have you on the team," I added cheerfully.

Charles's face flooded with relief. "Honestly?" he asked. "Because it's kind of fun, to tell you the truth."

I can't believe that I've avoided my sister's friends for

years, I thought, *and now I'm crushing on this guy who thinks Big Think is "fun"!*

I still was, though, more and more every minute I stood next to him. "Yeah," I said. "It's always good to have new competition—it keeps you sharp."

Charles nodded. "That's really true," he said. "I mean, I—I think that too," he stammered. I put my elbows down on the lab table and gave him a big, dizzying grin.

Charles froze, his hand on the coil of the Bunsen burner. "Oh, hey, I'm sorry!" he suddenly said, looking down at the experiment he had neatly assembled. "I'm totally hogging all the lab."

I almost burst out laughing. How could you hog a *lab?* It wasn't exactly the last slice of pizza.

"That's all right," I said dismissively. "I'm sick of these anyway."

Charles looked confused. He pushed his glasses up again and fumbled with the "retort," whatever that was. "But you did so well on the chemistry stuff the other day," he said.

"That's why I'm sick of it," I agreed immediately. I was doing exactly what Barry had taught us—rolling with the punches. "If you seem like you mean it," Barry was always saying, "it doesn't really matter if what you're saying doesn't make sense. So say it big!" Then he would spread his arms wide, like a gymnast after a vault.

"Well, we're almost done anyway," Charles said, leaning back down over the notebook and making some notations. *Thank my lucky stars,* I thought, glad that I had passed whatever test playing Ivory was. Trying to look somewhat interested in what was going on, I leaned down to look into the vial and sniffed.

I leaned back immediately, my eyes watering. It was like I had swallowed fire. I started to cough and couldn't stop.

"Hey, don't get too close to that!" Charles said. "That's sulfuric acid!"

My nose was burning. I ran over to the sink and frantically splashed water all over my face, trying to rid my nasal passages of the sensation that they had just been shot through with chili peppers. *Great, Ebony,* I said to myself. *Now you've burned your sister's nose off.*

Mr. Rosner was suddenly behind me. "Ivory, are you doing all right?" he asked.

I started to wipe my face with the roller cloth. After repeated flushings the sensations had finally subsided. "I . . . um . . . sniffed the wrong vial," I said, blowing my nose to try to get the last hint of burning out of my throat.

Mr. Rosner rocked back and forth on his heels and looked at me strangely, like he hoped I was joking. "Well, let's try not to sniff *any* test tubes, shall we?" he asked, clapping me on the back so that I started coughing again and had to drink another whole cup of water to calm down.

Everyone had started moving back to the front of the room, handing in their labs to Mr. Rosner on the way out. I staggered back to the table to retrieve mine. Charles was still standing there.

"I . . . um . . . penciled in all your answers," he said worriedly. "Since you were kinda indisposed."

"Thanks," I said, with more genuine relief than Charles knew. What a sweetie pie. And a lifesaver.

As we handed our labs to Mr. Rosner and made our way into the hall, I started to give Charles a little wave good-bye. He stopped me.

"Ivory, would you like to have lunch today?" he asked me.

I felt a buzz rise from my toes to my head. Even though I had been the worst lab partner in the world, he had asked me to *lunch. I knew this switching thing was a good idea!* I told myself triumphantly.

Unfortunately, Ivory and I had already agreed to meet for lunch the night before. This was both so that we wouldn't be stuck talking to each other's friends in any big way and also so that we could check in and "abort the mission" if necessary.

In a sense, I was relieved. I didn't want to push my luck with Charles right away.

"I'm . . . um . . . eating lunch with my sister today," I said, realizing that it was the first true thing I'd said in hours. "We, uh, like to catch up every once in a while."

Charles gave me a weird look, then laughed. "Okay," he said. "I'll see you at practice then, okay?" He clapped his hand on my shoulder, left it there for a second, and then walked down the hall with Peter.

At that moment I didn't care whether the whole plan blew up in my face. I didn't care whether I was never able to wear my red cowboy boots again. He was so cute, and he had asked me to lunch!

He had touched my shoulder.

I floated all the way to the cafeteria.

Eight

Charles

ALL THROUGH LUNCH I kept thinking about Ivory's 180-degree change from the previous days.

"What do you think happened?" I asked as Peter and I slid our trays onto a side table. "Do you think this is all part of some master plan?"

Peter snorted and glanced toward the center of the room. "Ivory's not that good of an actress," he said.

I looked at the table where she was sitting. Ivory was actually with a bunch of girls—Pria, some Asian girl, a girl with really curly blond hair, and one other girl that I assumed must be her sister.

"She's cute," I commented, freaking myself out. Suddenly I was becoming one of the guys— commenting on girls, putting my hands on their shoulders. It was social osmosis or something.

Mom had been proved right.

"Who?" Peter said, looking up from his macaroni and cheese. *"Ivory?"*

"Ivory's not so bad," I commented, realizing that I really did think that was true. I thought of her warm brown eyes and big smile at the lab table. I mean, when she smiled, she almost looked like an entirely different girl.

That wasn't who I had been talking about, though.

"I can't look at any girl who wears headbands," Peter said. "I mean, I know I'm no Russell Crowe, but I don't make it worse by wearing high waters or anything."

I took a sip of juice and looked at Ivory's sister again. Her hair stood out in a wild crackle from her head, and she was dressed kind of wildly too—some kind of print skirt and boots. She was definitely very pretty. "I meant her sister," I explained.

Peter looked at me blankly, then grinned. "They're twins," he said.

I looked at him in disbelief, then back at the two girls. "Naw," I replied, shaking my head. Peter wasn't going to get me on this one.

But Peter was nodding. "They are *twins,* man. I thought you knew that!"

I shook my head again. "I didn't even know Ivory had a sister until today," I said. "Man, they do not look *anything* alike."

"I know," Peter said, glancing at them and

grinning. "When they were younger, you couldn't tell them apart. But now they dress really different. It's like their personalities made them look different too."

I looked at Ivory's sister again. She was sedately eating her lunch, nodding occasionally as Ivory waved her hands around. "She's kind of shy?" I asked.

Peter snorted into his milk. "Ebony? Shy?" he asked. "Ebony's about as shy as a B-12 bomber."

I looked at them again. "She's an *actress*," Peter said in a flutey high voice.

"Oh," I said, unable to take my eyes off the two of them. I kept switching their features in my head, trying to see if they really did match. It was the weirdest thing how—once you blanked out everything else—they did.

Otherwise Ebony and Ivory did not look *any* more alike than Peter and I did.

"Nice names," I said, cracking up. "What's up with that?"

Peter laughed. "Hippie parents," he said. "Imparting the spirit of brotherhood wherever they can."

I realized that even though Ivory's sister was cuter, it was Ivory who had gotten my attention today. Sniffing a vial of sulfuric acid! What had she been thinking? She was a very experienced chemist, I knew. Could I have possibly distracted her?

Don't get in above your head, Corey, I thought, wishing Mary Claire were here to give me an independent evaluation of the events of the past couple of days. *You've got some new friends—let's just leave it at that for now.*

"Some of Ebony's friends are kind of cute too," Peter said, practically sticking his head into the milk carton immediately after the words left his mouth. I ducked my head so he couldn't see my smile. Somehow I had suddenly gotten the sense that Peter and I were definitely practicing this "man-talk" thing on each other.

Trying to be subtle, I followed Peter's eyes to the table of girls. They were fixed squarely on the Asian girl, who looked small, wiry, and very pretty.

I suddenly realized where I had seen her before. She was on the front door of the Web site Peter had designed for the school. In fact, now that I thought about it, she was all over the Web site: reading something on a lectern, kicking a soccer ball, bending over a book with extreme concentration.

I coughed and looked back at my tray so that Peter wouldn't notice that I had smoked him out. I just hoped he hadn't noticed that I might be getting a small crush on . . . Ivory.

"Yeah," I said, crumbling a piece of corn bread over some creamed spinach and covering the whole thing with four crumpled napkins—my contribution to the aesthetic portion of the Roosevelt High eating experience. "So tell me more about what the actual Big Think is like," I requested, changing the subject to a much more important matter. "Do we have handheld buzzers or foot thingers?"

*　　　*　　　*

Big Think practice that afternoon went pretty much the same as it had Tuesday. After the pizza and soda we all took our places at the two long tables and Mr. Rosner started passing out the problem sets. "Why don't we do boy-girl today," he said, noticing that we were all sitting in the same seats we had on Tuesday. "Just for variety's sake."

Everyone got up and switched around like we were playing musical chairs. I couldn't help but pass around the same side of the table as Ivory on my way to the new one. I willed myself not to get all shy and look away when we got close. Then, as we passed each other, we both looked up and smiled at the same second. I felt a little trill of excitement.

Yesterday you hated this girl! I thought. *How could you make such a big flip in twenty-four hours?*

But whatever I was feeling, it was out of my control.

I was just glad that whatever was happening between me and Ivory didn't seem, if you observed outside elements rationally and logically, to all be generated from the central region of my cerebral cortex.

Which is another way of saying that I hoped it wasn't all in my head.

We all finally got settled. I had already decided that I wasn't going to be so reserved today—especially since Ivory had given me the go-ahead in chemistry by saying she was glad to have me on the team. By the time Pria had passed out the pencils, I was drumming my fingers with excitement. No matter how fast Ivory answered any of the questions, I was going to be sure to answer them faster. It was time to take her at her word.

Mr. Rosner began clicking on his stopwatch. "Nine," I said, raising my hand on each question as quickly as I could. "Infinity." "Milwaukee, Wisconsin."

By the time we got to the fifth problem, though, I realized that competition from Ivory wasn't going to be much of a problem. I had gotten them all right so far, except for one in which I called out the radius, forgetting that the question had asked for the circumference. (Once you'd opened your mouth, you couldn't take back an answer, even if you realized it was wrong as you were uttering it.) But Ivory hadn't called out on a single one, even ones that I knew she could have done practically as fast as I had done them.

I looked across at Ivory. She seemed to sense my gaze and looked up right away. She gave me a little smile and a wave. I smiled back, then started to blush and looked down.

Was Ivory sitting out her round, just like I had sat out my first round?

I tried to concentrate on the next problem Rosner had passed out, but I was too late. Someone else called out the answer. Pria.

And she got it right.

After that, I was so rattled by what might have been Ivory's secret message to me that I couldn't concentrate on anything. Was she really not answering questions as a kind of joke on my behavior at the last practice? And if so, what did that mean?

Except that she definitely didn't hate me anymore.

Someone else called out the answer: another girl. Peter nudged me. "C'mon, man," he said. "You're going to let the girls whip our butts."

That's okay with me, I wanted to say. I was so jittery, I was afraid to look in Ivory's direction.

She still hadn't answered one question.

It was five to four, with the girls' team winning. "We're counting on you, dude," Peter muttered in mock threat, smiling into his sheet.

I looked down at the problem, but the words seemed to swim before me. Some train was going somewhere. . . . Some boat was going in the other direction. . . . Some current was running at seven miles an hour. . . . I couldn't keep it straight.

"Answer!" Peter yelled right next to me, making me jump.

Mr. Rosner looked up. He'd definitely given up on me, I could tell—decided I was one of those fickle geniuses who couldn't be trusted in a pinch.

Which, frankly, was turning out to be true.

Peter was reading something off his sheet. "The baker would get there at six in the morning," he said. "The candlestick maker two hours later."

Mr. Rosner looked like Regis Philbin about to ask if that was someone's final answer. "On what day?" he intoned.

Peter paled. "Thursday," he finally burst out.

Mr. Rosner clicked the timer. "Correct," he

said, and leaned down to mark the scores on his notepad.

Peter leaned over to whisper to me. "That was a total guess, man," he said. "But I took one for the team."

"Sorry, man," I whispered back. "I got distracted."

"Uh-huh," Peter said, grinning at me and stroking his chin.

Ivory started to answer a lot more questions as the match wound down. By the time we got to literature, she was buzzing along, going head-to-head with Peter for most of the answers while the rest of us sat there, always a second or two too late with our responses.

"The author of *What Maisie Knew*?"

"The brother in *To Kill a Mockingbird*?"

"The creature to whom the phrase `darkness visible' refers?"

"The setting of Sinclair Lewis's *Main Street*?"

Finally Peter gave up and gave the stage to Ivory. She ran roughshod over all of us, finishing the round at least twenty points ahead of anyone else.

"Wow, Ivory never does this well in literature," Peter said, impressed. "This was a hard round too. She must have been reading up."

I was impressed too. The only girl I could think of who could have done as well as Ivory just had was, of course, Mary Claire.

But then again, Mary Claire was a genius.

And what good was it being a genius if you couldn't even keep your mind on the game?

"Miss Marple," Ivory snapped happily to the last question, and practice was over.

I tapped Peter on the arm. "I'm going to go talk to Ivory a sec," I said. "See you later, okay?"

Peter cocked an eyebrow. "Good to see you two getting along," he said, slinging his backpack over his shoulder as he headed out and giving me a little salute.

I was too intent on making sure Ivory didn't slip out ahead of me to worry about whether that meant Peter had figured out anything about my sudden crush. Even if he had, I wasn't too worried. If he was going to tease me about Ivory, I could definitely tease him back about . . . what was her name again? Web-site girl.

I went right over to Ivory like I was being cranked in by an invisible winch. I couldn't help it. "Ivory," I said, catching her jacket sleeve just before she marched out the door.

"Charles," she said, her eyes wide behind her glasses, smiling. "Good game!"

"Tuesday, math, Thursday, literature, huh?" I asked, trying to sound jaunty. It was coming out more dorky, I was sure, but I couldn't give up on the joke now that I had started it. "What are you going to tackle next week—fly-fishing?"

Ivory tried to look modest. "I've been reading a lot lately," she said. "Those questions just happened to be about a lot of the books I *just* read."

I had the feeling Ivory was only trying to make me feel better for not knowing any of the answers, practically. "You just read thirty-four books?" I asked. "You must be a speed reader."

"Well, you know," Ivory said. She was definitely blushing—even I could tell. Was it me? Or was she just shy? "I guess I'm a little quicker than other people," Ivory said.

That gave me the courage to say what I said next. Believe me, it was the first time I had ever said those words in my life. But then, I had had a lot of firsts over the past couple of days.

"Wanna go to a movie?" I asked.

We wound up at the Senator, an old theater Ivory steered us to, the only one within walking distance from the school. On the way over, Ivory kept up a constant stream of chatter about her past, most of which involved her sister.

". . . and then we went to Camp Saratoga and learned to sail. Ebony was the better swimmer, but I learned how to flip a kayak first. . . ."

". . . my mom and dad thought Ebony and Ivory would be cute names. That was way, way before the song, but that's no excuse, in my opinion. . . ."

". . . my sister is a really good actress. We're complete opposites in almost every way, but I really love her a lot. It would be weird if we were exactly the same, I think. Don't you? . . ."

I listened intently, finding it hard to reconcile the dour girl of my first day with this animated, bubbly spitfire. *Ivory must keep all this under wraps,* I thought. *She only shows her true self when she really is sure that she wants to get to know another person.*

I was just glad that she was showing her true self because I certainly liked it a lot better than the one who had hated my guts.

"You don't look anything like your sister," I finally offered. "It's weird that you're identical twins."

Ivory looked up at me shyly—or maybe it was just her glasses that made her look shy. "We're different," she said in what sounded like an almost defiant tone. "Ebony is really—"

"I don't want to hear about Ebony," I broke in a little hurriedly. I gulped. "I didn't mean that I don't want to hear about your sister," I explained, babbling at a mile a minute to make up for any perceived rudeness. "I just meant, not until I know more about you," I lamely explained.

Ivory gave me a huge smile. Then, like a sudden storm cloud, it was replaced by a really fearful look. Then the sun broke behind the clouds, and she gave me a small, crooked grin.

"Did you . . . um . . . *always* want to get to know me better?" she asked softly.

I was so relieved that Ivory wasn't mad about the sister thing that I did something else that I'd certainly never done. It just happened, like all of the other things that had been happening lately.

I actually took her hand.

"To tell you the truth, I was kind of scared by

you at first," I said. "But I'm not anymore," I said, giving her hand a squeeze.

Now Ivory smiled a *real* smile—that big, great smile that I had first seen at our lab table. "Here we are," she said, jerking her head toward the movie marquee, lit up behind her like a corona of fireworks.

Nine

Ebony

BY THE TIME I got home from my date with Charles, let me list for you the things that I did not care about:

1. I did not care that Ivory's headband was eating through my head the way the sulfuric acid had almost eaten through my nose earlier;
2. I did not care that Ivory's jeans, which were much stiffer and newer than any kind I ever wore, had rubbed my legs so much that I was sure they would be covered with a million little red bumps when I finally yanked them off;
3. I did not care that even though I had just had an incredibly romantic first date, I had no way to tell Charles that the girl he'd just gone to see *Annie Hall* with wasn't the girl he thought she was;
4. I did not care that I hadn't done any of my homework.

Here are the things that I *did* care about, also in no particular order:

1. That Charles had asked me to the movies;
2. That Charles had held my hand;
3. That Charles bought me ice cream at Stewart's;
4. That I whupped Charles's butt at practice.

Charles had also walked me home, but I decided not to count that since it was pretty clear that Charles was still totally lost in our town. Before we said good night, I'd had to take the old scraggly napkin from the restaurant out of my pocket and mark down rough directions to his street for him.

"No sense of direction, huh?" I asked.

"Not much," Charles answered, smiling with embarrassment. "Thanks."

I had the sense that if I waited one more second, Charles would try to kiss me. But then I got nervous.

"See ya," I said, waving.

"See ya," he answered, setting off down the darkening street.

It was about seven o'clock. Luckily Mom and Dad still weren't home from work. And if Ivory asked why I was getting home so late, I'd just tell her . . . *something*. I'd made up my mind not to tell her about Charles and Annie Hall. I ran upstairs to my room to shower and change, wild to hear about how Ivory's day had gone as *me*.

I burst into my room. Ivory was sitting on my bed, looking at the door like she'd been staring at it for hours. She was all dressed back in her old stuff already—she'd even already straightened her hair again.

"Hey, there can't be two of us in the same room at the same time," I joked. "A hole is going to open in the space-time continuum or something."

Ivory didn't laugh. "Eb," she said, her brow furrowed. "I've got some really bad news."

I sat down on the bed and put my arm around her. Maybe now she'd finally tell me what was going on. I hoped no one had been hurt or anything. "Ivory," I said with concern. "Is everything all right?"

Ivory sighed. "It's about me," she said. "And you."

This is the way the total destruction of all my hopes and dreams happened, exactly as Ivory told it to me:

Dev and Olivia had been really nice today, Ivory said, and actually they had found some things in common to talk about. And it had been fun being me—even if my boots were kind of uncomfortable. (My western boots definitely didn't fit me either, but I liked them so much that I wasn't willing to give them up.) People reacted to her a little differently—instead of almost looking through her when she walked down the hall, they had smiled and said hello.

"I didn't realize I had so many friends," I said weakly.

"Just wait," Ivory said, sending my stomach

plummeting into my shoes. Had she told Dev or Olivia some flippant comment I'd made about them or something? Were my best friends no longer speaking to me? That would be unbelievably awful—and ironic, as Ms. Cabral would add.

Then Ivory shot me a glance. "You might not know it," she said softly, "but you practically know everybody in that school."

Except for Charles, until today, I thought.

"Ivory, you *have* to get to the point," I said in desperation. "I'm so worried, I'm about to crack this headband in two."

"Don't do that," Ivory said, lifting the headband from my hair much more gently than I had combed hers yesterday. Then she placed it in her lap and continued.

After lunch she'd had to go alone to drama with Barry since neither Dev nor Olivia had that class. She was a little worried about it since she'd never been in a drama class before. She knew we did all sorts of exercises like falling back into some other person's arms (to get us to trust each other) and shouting at the tops of our lungs (to get the willies out).

I suddenly realized what must have happened— Ivory had had to get up onstage or something, and she had succumbed to stage fright. "What happened—did he make you read and you puked or something?" I said sympathetically. I'd seen a bunch of people do that before, and believe me—you never get over losing your cookies in front of thirty other people.

130

As Barry would say, it's "a growth experience."

Ivory shook her head deliberately, as if it hurt her neck to do it. "Not exactly," she said.

Ivory continued with her story, which was as gripping as some horror movie at this point. The class had been embarking on the second read through of *Twelfth Night* when the thing that Ivory had been most afraid of happened. Barry had called on "me."

He had asked her to read the main role: Viola, the girl who dressed as a boy to work for the Count Orsino under the name Cesario.

"I thought that was really funny," Ivory said, "because of how we were switching places too."

I nodded weakly, too afraid to speak. Had Ivory done such a bad job that I'd been kicked out of Proscenium or something? That didn't seem possible. Some of the people who loved drama the most—and Barry—sometimes sounded like they were reading the phone book when Barry made them get up and try out a role.

"So I tried to do the best I could," Ivory continued. "And I thought I had done okay. We went on for a really long time, though—Barry didn't let us stop until the bell rang."

So what had happened? I was beside myself. "Barry does that sometimes," I said cautiously, "if he feels that people are working really well together."

Ivory looked up at me, a miserable expression on her face. That was when the *oh-no* bell began clanging in my head. I couldn't believe the words

131

were true until I heard them from Ivory's lips, though.

"So," Ivory continued, looking down at her dangling feet and swinging them against the bed rail, "I was just leaving class when Barry told me to stay behind for a second."

I couldn't say anything.

Ivory looked up at me, and I realized she had small tears beginning in the corners of her eyes. "I really didn't mean to do it, Ebony," she said. "It wasn't deliberate or anything!"

My limbs felt like they were made of lead. "Go on," I said.

Ivory looked down at her feet again.

"At first I was worried that Barry had figured out what we were doing," she said. "I mean, he is the drama teacher, after all. And it's not like I'm a very good actress. Or I thought I wasn't," she said, laughing weakly and shaking her head.

Please, please don't let what I think this is be true, I thought frantically.

"So when he talked to me, Barry said that I'd made a more radical improvement than he'd ever seen anyone make in his entire career," Ivory said, almost inaudibly.

"Uh-huh," I said, unable to believe what seemed to be happening.

"And he said," Ivory continued, her voice cracking a little, "that even though I was only a sophomore, he was going to do something he'd never done before."

"Uh-huh," I said again, like a robot.

Ivory looked up at me again. "Ebony, don't be mad at me!" she cried. "I really didn't mean it!"

"Of course you didn't," I said coldly. I wanted to plunge my head into my pillows and wake up from the conversation hours later, as if it had all been a bad dream.

"And he said," Ivory finally got out, "that even though auditions weren't until next week, he was sure of one thing."

"And what was that?" I asked, even though I already knew.

Ivory tried to look me in the eyes, but I couldn't look at her. Finally she gave up and stared off into the distance.

"That he wanted me to play Viola in the spring play," Ivory said.

I could feel my heart beating in my chest. If it got louder, I thought crazily, it might block out everything Ivory was saying.

"That's not all," Ivory said.

Cold sweat was breaking up on my forehead. What else could she possibly have to tell me? That in the interests of Proscenium, I was never, ever going to be allowed back into the auditorium, not even for dumb assemblies?

"What is it?" I whispered.

Ivory's mouth turned down at the corners like a clown's. "He wanted to know," she said, "if my sister might be interested in playing Sebastian since it's such a small part. He thought—" Ivory covered her mouth for a second, than laughed mirthlessly. "He thought that it might be really cool to have Viola and Sebastian played by real twins."

*Ebony Swallows Her Pride and
Admits Her Life Is a Huge Mess,
Act 1, Scene 1*

EBONY: Well, you got the lead. You have to do it.

IVORY: I don't want to do it!

EBONY: [*happy but cautious*] Do you not want to do it because you hate acting? Or is it just because you're scared?

IVORY: [*practically inaudible*] I'm scared.

EBONY: [*feeling nauseated*] Ivory, you got the lead in the school play. You're going to do it.

IVORY: I'm scared to tell you the truth.

EBONY: What's the truth?

IVORY: [*really, really softly*] I kind of want to do it.

Then, although I wasn't even interested anymore, Ivory told me what had been bothering her for the past couple of days.

"You know Big Think's really important to me," Ivory said. She laughed ruefully. "I mean, let's face it: it's practically my whole social life. And when Rosner got so excited about Charles coming onto the team, I knew what was going to happen."

I was sitting next to her, thoughts whirling

134

around in my head so fast, I could barely stand it. I forced myself to pay attention.

"What was going to happen?" I managed to croak.

Ivory looked at me like I was the biggest idiot she'd ever seen. "Charles was going to be made captain, and I would lose my space on the team."

I got indignant. "Ivory, that's not true! I mean, you're practically Mr. Rosner's right-hand man. He'd never let the team go to Big Think without you."

Ivory looked at me like I was getting stupider with every passing minute. She shook her head. "My subjects are science and math," she said. "Charles finished those in fourth grade, right? There's no way I could ever compete with that."

But you can compete with me, I thought. *And win.*

"I know this is horrible, Ebony," she said. "But I was feeling so bad about myself until this happened—like I'd lost the thing I liked best in the world."

I know how you feel, I thought, wondering wildly why I hadn't just listened to Dev and Olivia's warnings in the first place.

"Now I feel so much better," Ivory said, smiling a little despite her sad expression. "I mean, that I'm good at something anyway."

I couldn't answer. I didn't know what to say.

Ivory, I wanted to ask. *Tell me something: how does that feel?*

I was lying in my bed, a pillow over my eyes. I had already told my mom and dad, separately, that I was feeling really sick and didn't want to come down for dinner. My dad had brought up a tray with some tea and crackers, kissed my forehead, patted my shoulder, then left.

So let's get this straight, Ebony, I was telling myself over and over again. *In one day your sister has managed to get the lead in the school play, something you've been trying to do for the past two years. You also started a relationship with a guy who thinks that you're your sister—and who's going to figure out eventually that there's a reason that you practically stuck your head into a vat of acid this morning.*

When he finds out that you're not Ivory, he might actually wish that you had.

On the bright side, you have a role in the school play if you want it—because you happen to look exactly like someone who actually can *act.*

I rolled over on my stomach and groaned.

Ivory and I had decided, for the time being, we would have to keep switching until we figured out what to do. I couldn't exactly get up there and blow her cover, could I? When I tried to be Viola, Barry would wonder exactly what he had been thinking by giving me the role. And who knew what would happen then.

Also, now I couldn't just "slip" back into Ebony, like I had been planning to. It made it complicated enough that "Ivory" had already gone on a date with Charles, I realized—how had I been going to switch back now anyway? And now that Ivory had taken my place in Barry's class, we were going to have to think of some new plan. Unless I wanted to wear a headband for the rest of the year.

Isn't it enough that you made Ivory really supersmart? I asked the ceiling. *Does she have to be the "artistic" one too?*

Because—excuse me, but it's true—that's supposed to be my job!

Ten

Charles

WHEN I GOT home from my date with Ivory, Dad was hunched over the kitchen table, scribbling, and my mother was banging away at some Chopin, as usual.

"Dinner in an hour," my mother called out as I walked through the living room, not missing a note or changing tempo whatsoever. "Chinese or Indian?"

"Indian," I called back, too buzzed from my date with Ivory to even mind that it was the fourth time that week we'd had takeout—and the second time we'd had Indian.

Annie Hall had been playing at the Senator. I'd already seen it a million times with my mom, but since it was one of the greatest movies of all time, I didn't mind seeing it again. Even if it's about a romance that doesn't work out, it's still a great date movie.

Ivory had seen it before too, and she giggled at all the right parts, once cracking up so loudly that the only other people in the theater—a grizzled couple who looked like they'd been sitting there since 1955—turned around and glared at her until she stopped.

"This is very serious theater," I whispered to her. "No fooling around."

"Silent movies," Ivory muttered back, making me crack up too.

When we'd said good-bye, I'd really wanted to give her a good-night kiss. Ivory slipped away before I could get up the courage. That was okay—it might have thrown me over my limit for things-I've-never-done-before-but-I'm-doing-today-for-some-reason.

To be honest, I wasn't even *sure* how you gave a girl a kiss. Did you just lunge forward, or did you ask if you could kiss her? Which annoyed girls more?

Which made them think you were a big dork?

This was something Pebbles507 was sure to know from reading all those novels.

I went up to my room and switched on the computer. There was an e-mail from Peter waiting in my in box.

From: Penrightman@aol.com
To: CoreyFlakes@erols.com

Genius—
  Have you been tickling the Ivories?
                    Historian

I smiled and hit reply.

From: CoreyFlakes@erols.com
To: Penrightman@aol.com

No. But my mom is.

I started writing an e-mail to Mary Claire. She had just sent me this huge letter about her novel and all of the problems she was having with it. I was glad that our luck seemed to have switched for the time being since Mary Claire always landed on her feet. There was a JPEG attached to the e-mail with a drawing of her favorite hat—a big, black lacy thing that was only appropriate for Halloween.

From: CoreyFlakes@erols.com
To: Pebbles507@aol.com

Nice hat. Don't quit your day job, though.
Remember what I told you about that girl Ivory? Well, you're never going to believe this.

That was as far as I got before there was a knock at the door. It was my dad. "Charles?" he said. "You want chicken vindaloo or mutter paneer?" he asked, naming my two favorite dishes of all time.
"Vindaloo," I called back, typing away.
I could tell that Dad was still outside my door.

"Mom says you got a letter," he said through the wood. "Do you want to come down and get it?"

I stopped typing. "A letter?" I asked.

It was a thin, white envelope, sitting on the mail table. (I never sifted through the mail—since we moved so often, we hardly ever got any anyway. It was mostly solicitations and big bulky packages from work for my dad.)

I picked it up. It had been sent to our old address, but the yellow forwarding sticker had gotten it here a day or two after the first postmark.

The return address was Rush Creek.

Dad had wandered off into the kitchen. I could hear him reading off from the menu to whoever was at the other end of the phone call. "Two orders of samosas . . . one dal . . . one lamb biryani . . ."

I couldn't wait one more second. I ripped open the envelope and shook out the thin piece of paper.

Dear Charles Corey, the first line read.

We are very pleased to welcome you to the graduating class of 2005 at Rush Creek School of the Arts. . . .

I walked into the living room and finished the letter with trembling hands. I had gotten it all: full scholarship, room and board, and the option to come in September or defer for a year if I wanted.

"Charles?" Dad said from the doorway of the living room. He'd hung up the phone. "Anything important?"

I felt a warm rush to my head. Last week this letter had been all I wanted in the world. Now I didn't know how to feel.

"Yeah," I said slowly. "Can I talk to you and Mom?"

It took me a little while to explain what Rush Creek was—Mom had heard of it, but Dad didn't know anything about it. It took even longer to explain why I had applied in the first place.

"All this moving around means I can't make any friends," I said, trying to keep the anger out of my voice. "And everywhere I go, I just feel like a big freak—I mean, I don't even *have* to be in high school for academics. I already feel like I'm just marking time, and then you yank me out before I can put down any roots." I heaved a deep breath. "I'd probably do better as a traveling salesman."

Dad smiled, but my mom looked even more serious. "We know that was very hard for you to leave Mary Claire," my mom observed. She and my dad looked at each other. "We've been thinking about that a lot, actually."

"Charles, we're sorry," my dad said. "If we'd known how much this was upsetting you, we'd have tried to make other arrangements."

My mom nodded. "In fact, we've been talking about settling down here, at least until you graduate, so that what happened to you with Mary Claire won't keep happening," she said with worry.

I looked up. Could that be true? My mother's face was lined with anxiety. My father nodded at me, then sighed.

So my parents weren't quite as oblivious as I'd thought, I realized.

"And I don't approve of boarding schools," Dad added. "I mean, there's time enough for you to be out in the real world when you're eighteen. Your mother and I want you here with us."

"But I know what an opportunity this is," my mother said, getting a little teary eyed. "If you really feel strongly about it, Charles, your father and I won't stand in your way."

I couldn't believe it. They weren't screaming and telling me that there was no way I could go. They also weren't wandering off as if I had just announced I was going to make a tuna-fish sandwich for lunch. They were concerned, but they were letting me make my own decision. Like an adult.

That—along with so many other things—was new.

"I don't know if I want to go anymore," I confessed. "I'm starting to make some friends here, you know."

My mother's eyes lit up. "You are?" she asked. "You like the school?"

It felt weird to suddenly start telling my parents about my real life—normally I just let them wander around, and they let me wander around, and we were both *vague* with each other—the Vagabonds. It felt better to be getting into specifics. "Yeah," I admitted, thinking of Ivory and Peter.

"So, you think you might like to stay here if your mother and I made arrangements for that?"

Dad said, looking a little less unhappy. "Because to tell you the truth, I think your mother and I could use a rest too."

"I don't want you to think we weren't thinking of you all this time," my mother broke in. "Part of the reason we traveled so much when you were young was to expose you to new experiences: you were such a curious child, and we wanted to make the most out of that."

"Yeah," I finally said, cracking my knuckles with nervousness. "I know." Suddenly, I realized, I did. I should have known better than to convince myself for all these years that my parents were only moving around so much because they didn't care about me. I mean, there they were, right across from me on the couch—where they always were. I thought about how much they were always home with me too. How many kids had I heard of where both parents worked until ten, and they mostly had the remote and the Internet for company?

"They said I could defer for a year anyway," I told my parents.

My parents both look thrilled. The doorbell rang, and Dad got up to pay the deliveryman. As he spread the cartons around the dinner table and we sat down, Dad offered one last word on Rush Creek.

"Well, defer until after dinner anyway." He smiled, passing me the rice. "You don't want to make any decisions on an empty stomach."

Eleven

Ebony

THE NEXT MORNING I put on my headband like it was a crown of iron spikes, miserably thinking I'd never been so glad to have a Friday come in my life.

Last night Ivory and I had agreed not to change anything until the weekend came. Tomorrow and Sunday we would sit down and figure out what to do to clean up the big mess I'd dumped all over our lives.

It wasn't simple enough for both of us just to confess the truth to Barry. Although he probably would have thought it was funny, people would still wonder how the unknown Ivory had risen to the starring role out of nowhere when it was her sister who was supposed to be the great actress. I mean, Barry could have her officially audition, but Proscenium members would recognize her great performance as "mine" from the day before—and wonder what the hell was going on.

The Charles Corey angle wasn't particularly simple either. I must have had sulfuric acid still wafting around in my head when I'd agreed to go to the movies with him—even when I'd waved to him at Big Think practice! I'd just wanted to check him out from close up to make sure I wouldn't have a repeat of the jerk-alert Jason Warshof debacle. Now, I realized, all I'd done was give Charles Corey a big crush on my *sister*. Did I think it wasn't going to be a little awkward to get it back from her?

I covered my face with my hands. Perhaps Ivory would agree to tell everyone that this "twin" thing was all a big hoax—it had always been just *her* playing both girls all along. Then she could do the play, Big Think, and date Charles. And if hundreds of people hadn't seen us standing together for years and years, if there weren't reams and reams of videotapes and hundreds of photographs of us together, it would have been a really feasible idea.

I certainly wasn't adding anything to our magnificent duo lately.

I sighed and dragged myself downstairs to breakfast and Ivory's backpack, which she had retrieved and filled with her neatly done homework, I was sure. I hadn't done anything with mine—certainly I hadn't written a word ever since Ivory and I had talked last night. But even if she had stolen my role in the play, I didn't need to give Ivory her first set of tardies on top of everything else.

For the first couple of periods I hauled myself around like a big truckful of dirt. Pria, sensing that something was up, withdrew and didn't bug me. I was incredibly grateful—I was just worried about what I was going to do when I finally saw Charles. Should I act like I hated him again so that he would be more receptive to "Ebony" if she ever reappeared? Should I just act normal? Neutral?

I wanted to scream.

But by the time we got to chemistry, it turned out that I had nothing to worry about. I didn't even look in Charles and Peter's direction when I came in. And the minute everyone sat down, Mr. Rosner handed out a pop quiz on the last unit. "Get started, people," he said, clicking on his ubiquitous stopwatch.

What was I even doing here? I couldn't help thinking as I looked down at the rows and rows of neatly typed questions. I was supposed to be reciting the lines of *Twelfth Night* or hanging out with Ms. Cabral and Olivia, eating Twinkies and drinking Tab while we talked about the latest book she had just recommended for us. I was not supposed to be calculating moles and molecules and grams of H_2O.

I steeled myself to not turn around and look at Charles.

Because if I did turn around—if he did look up and smile at me—he would be smiling at the wrong person.

I spent the lunch hour gazing at the far door of a stall in the bathroom. Even though I knew that Dev and Olivia would be wild to know what was going on, I just couldn't face them. Pria and Ivory could spill all the beans and the four of them could put two and two together, as far as I was concerned. Playing someone else had given me a really uncomfortable sense of how shaky everything I had based my identity on at Roosevelt High was anyway.

Let's face the truth, Ebony, I told myself, drumming my feet against the far door. *You thought that playing someone else for a day would give you more control in a relationship. But actually, you've given up any control you ever could have had.*

And a role in the school play, I added disconsolately.

The bell rang, and the bathroom was flooded with girls. Hoping I wouldn't see anyone I knew, I pushed my way out of the crush.

Wait a minute. "Ivory" hardly knew anyone. I didn't have to worry about blending in with the crowd anymore.

Without thinking, I started walking toward the drama room. How hard had it been for Ivory, all of these years, feeling that her sister had so many more friends than she did? That her sister was always kind of looking down on her? Making fun of her?

I clutched my books closer to my chest. *Ivory probably felt a lot like I feel right now,* I thought, noticing that guilt as well as misery was now welling up in my gut. *The lamest of the lame.*

The second bell rang, and the last students straggled into their classrooms. All the doors closed. I sank to a seat on the empty stairwell.

Not that I think it's payback or anything, I thought, a headache forming behind my eyes like a ball-peen hammer was tapping a steady hole in my skull. *But it might be nice if you tried to feel glad for Ivory, Ebony— not just jealous.*

I had another thought—one that made me feel a hundred times guiltier than I already did. *Because I think if you hadn't been so mean about how dorky she was before, you wouldn't be so freaked out that she's a better actress than you now.*

I took a few deep breaths. *I mean, you might be a little jealous of someone else, Ebony, right?* I thought. *But you wouldn't begrudge a "nondork" the part, would you?*

Trying to be as quiet as possible, I sneaked down the stairs and walked toward the drama room. Even if I had wanted to go to Ivory's class, for the life of me, I couldn't remember where she was supposed to be at that moment.

Only where *I* was supposed to be—the old me.

Although one part of me knew exactly what I had come to see, another part of me wished desperately that all the students in Barry's class were just lying around in a circle, humming, or pretending to be wind and fire. Then I wouldn't have to face my worst fear.

I peeked into the classroom. They weren't pretending to be wind and fire.

Through the small glass window I could see Ivory, Wallace, and a few other seniors standing in front of the class. They were all reading from the play while the class—its back to me—watched in respectful silence.

"O time! thou must untangle this, not I," Ivory was saying as I opened the door a crack, trying not to make any noise. No one noticed. "It is too hard a knot for me to untie!" Then all the actors sighed and looked up—that was clearly the end of the scene.

"Okay, people," Barry said. "That was excellent, Ebony. Good work."

My throat was dry. I tried to swallow anyway. *Too big a knot for me to untangle is right,* I thought.

"Let's run through it again," Barry said.

All the actors relaxed and shrugged, then picked up their scripts. I could barely breathe while I waited for Ivory to start again.

"You either fear his humor or my negligence, that you call into question the continuance of his love: is he inconstant, sir, in his favors?" Ivory was answering as the actors moved around at the front of the room. Wallace spoke back to her in loud, angry strokes. I watched the scene unfold again, then turned back into the hall, letting the door close behind me.

One part of me still felt the same as I had before: angry, jealous, deep in the pits of hell. Another part of me was totally amazed by what I had just seen.

It was incredible. Even in the few minutes I had been watching Ivory, one thing was clear, and I would never, ever think of my sister in the same way again:

Ivory was a really *excellent* actress.

I don't mean that she was a good actress or that you just liked to watch her on the stage. But in those few moments that she stood up, simply reading from a half-folded book, she wasn't even my sister. She was Viola, the girl who had dressed up as someone else to figure out who she was going to be in the world.

I thought about our first reading of the play and how at the time it had struck me as such a cute idea—just to switch places with my sister for a second to see if the guy I liked was really as great as I thought. But Viola hadn't wanted to be someone else to sneak around or to play a trick on someone else. She had only dressed in costume to get a job.

I let my book bag drop on the floor. I had to smile, even though I felt sadder than I ever had for as long as I could remember.

Was I going to be able to figure out who I was in the world too?

I started down the hall toward Ivory's class, thinking that whatever happened, we were going to go back to ourselves right away. And I was going to come clean to whoever I had to in order to set all this straight. Even Charles Corey. I had been really stupid, but it wasn't the worst thing in the world. The next time I wouldn't be so stupid.

I racked my brains. What was Ivory's class again—what was it? Physics? English, with Ms. Cabral?

I was just fumbling in my knapsack for Ivory's schedule when the PA system crackled to life.

"Will the following students please come to the office," Dr. Guess's secretary said. "Pria Maramongolem, Ebony Thomas, Ivory Thomas, Peter Enright, Charles Corey, and Lucas Townsend."

I literally almost jumped a foot in the air, looking around me in panic. Why would Dr. Guess be calling us all to the office? What could be happening? I hadn't imagined the whole thing. Had I?

From the stairwell I saw the door to the drama room open. There was Ivory, looking almost exactly like *me,* making her way to Dr. Guess's office.

So it hadn't been my imagination.

I felt the heebie-jeebies start to rise in my stomach again. There was absolutely no reason for Dr. Guess to be calling every single one of us into his office.

Unless he had found out about my plan.

I felt my legs turn to rice pudding as I looked around for an escape route. Just what was Dr. Guess going to make me do? Confess and apologize to Charles? Just how many more humiliations was I going to be made to experience in one short week?

And how had he found out about the whole thing in the first place?

Maybe Shannon told him, I thought, wildly trying to think of (*a*) who could have found out about the switch and (*b*) who hated me enough to tell on me. Or could it have been Peter? He had known Ivory and me for most of our lives—and that would explain why he was in the office too.

But why would Peter possibly care? He was Charles's friend, I knew, but it still seemed like a long shot from his red hair and sticking-out ears to Dr. Guess's office.

And what the heck did this "Lucas Townsend" have to do with anything?

As I walked slowly down the stairs, various scenarios whipped around in my head, each increasingly ridiculous. Lucas Townsend was a jealous actor who had found out about me and Ivory and was trying to knock us out of the play so he could play Sebastian, Viola's lost brother. Charles had known all along and had told Dr. Guess the whole story to get me and my sister kicked out of school. Pria had decided she hated both me and Ivory and so had arranged a secret meeting for our double humiliation.

The most ridiculous scenario was that Dr. Guess would actually call us into his office for something as stupid as Ivory and me switching places for one day.

Still, I couldn't shake it from my head.

My footsteps rang in the empty corridor. Each step, I was sure, brought me closer to my doom.

When I entered the office, the secretary looked up with a smile. They were trained to do that, though. "Well, hello, Ivory!" she said. "Dr. Guess is waiting with the rest of the students in his office. Just go right in."

My entire diaphragm felt like it would shatter into a thousand pieces if I so much as allowed myself a real, deep breath.

Now, remember, I told myself. *If it comes down to the actual facts, just claim amnesia. Rules 2 and 3: Never apologize, never explain.*

I touched the heavy oak door, and it swung open. Greeting me were the faces of my sister, Charles, Peter Enright, Pria, and some black-haired boy I didn't know. They all looked as confused and expectant as I was.

When I got the courage to look in Dr. Guess's face, I was surprised to see that he was beaming at me.

Maybe he had just lost his mind?

"Ivory," he boomed, coming over and leading me to the one empty chair in the office. "So glad you're here." He swept back into his leather chair and looked at us all with a satisfied grin. "Now we can begin." He smiled.

I could feel Ivory—the *real* Ivory—shooting a glance my way, and I looked up. *What's going on?* her worried expression seemed to say.

Ivory, do I look like I know any more than you do? I tried to telepathically transmit back.

Charles looked at me and gave me a hesitant smile. This time I was too terrified to smile back. I was glad Ivory's glasses practically hid half my face—I wished I could crawl under the chair and hide under it. I clutched my backpack and waited for the ax to fall.

"So," Dr. Guess said, emphatically placing his hands on the table. "I'm sure you're all wondering why I've called you to the office today."

Isn't it funny how any strange situation will bring out the guilt lurking in someone? I thought, noticing that everyone looked at least as nervous and jittery as I did. *But I'm sure I have a lot more to feel guilty about,* I added hastily to myself.

"Well," Dr. Guess said, pulling a manila folder off his desk, "I am very pleased to inform you that you have all been chosen to represent Roosevelt High at the Big Think meet this May."

There was complete silence. Finally Dr. Guess just laughed at us. "Or shall I say, you've all earned yourselves a spot on the team," he said proudly. He took out a piece of paper and brought it closer to his glasses so that he could read the small print. "Charles, in math, of course. Peter . . ." He looked at him over the top of his glasses. "History. Pria and Ivory," he said, glancing at me, "you've tied for the top space in the sciences, and Ebony," he said, looking at Ivory, "I'm very happy to report that you have scored the highest in literature. And Lucas," he said, glancing at the rest of us. "Lucas is only a freshman!" He chortled. "Lucas will be representing our school in languages."

He looked around at all of us proudly. Still complete silence.

"Well." Dr. Guess finally laughed again. "Don't any of you have anything to say?"

Twelve

Charles

PRIA WAS THE first one to answer Dr. Guess.

I had to admit, when we got to Dr. Guess's office, I was just glad to see Ivory. (Of course, I'd been called to the principal's office enough in my life that I wasn't really worried about it. It never, ever was because I'd started a fight in the lunchroom, you know?) In class we had been given a pop quiz, and then she had rushed out. I had planned to try to talk to her at lunch, but I didn't see her anywhere in the lunchroom—she definitely wasn't at the table with her sister, Olivia, Pria, and that blond girl whose name I couldn't remember.

Was she mad at me because of yesterday? Maybe she'd thought better of it and didn't want any kind of friendship, let alone relationship.

Maybe that girl I had met yesterday had just disappeared, along with all of my hopes for this school.

Sitting there in the office, with Ivory refusing to even look at me, I started to get nervous.

Still, I wasn't surprised that she'd been picked for the Big Think team. I mean, who else if not her? Peter had clearly been a shoo-in too. I wasn't surprised to see that her sister, Ebony, was also really smart—both of them must be really big readers. If she was anywhere near as good as Ivory, she would sweep all the questions at the meet.

We all turned to see what Pria had to say.

"I'm really sorry," Pria said. "But I don't think I'm going to be able to do it."

Ivory's sister turned to Dr. Guess. "Actually, I don't think I'll be able to do it either."

Dr. Guess laughed—but it wasn't a happy laugh this time. He looked from Pria to Ebony, who was looking more and more agitated with each second. "This is a very big honor, you know." He laughed again, very uncomfortably. "Why, I don't know if we've even picked alternates!"

Nobody said anything. Finally Pria spoke again.

"Dr. Guess, I'm very sorry," she said. "But I'm going to be spending all my time helping my friend with a special project."

Dr. Guess looked dubiously at Pria, then at Ebony. Ebony gave Pria a questioning look, and

Pria shook her head, as if to say, *Not you.* Peter and I looked at each other—*Is this normal?* I asked; *Not at all,* he seemed to be saying back—and then back at Dr. Guess.

"And you, Ebony?" Dr. Guess asked, looking more and more irritated with every passing second.

Ebony looked at Ivory, and she looked back. "I'm—I'm going to be in the school play," she said slowly. "I'm going to be in rehearsals every night, and I—"

"So we've got an actress and a 'special-projects' coordinator," said Dr. Guess. He turned to the rest of us. "Do we have any other defectors?" he snapped. I looked at Ivory, but she was still looking away from me.

Dr. Guess leaned down to make a notation on the sheet. "Well, at least we have you, Ivory," he said, giving her a cursory nod. "You'll handle chemistry, biology, and physics. I believe Olivia MacDougal was the second-highest scorer in the literature section of the test—Nancy?" he called to the outer office. His secretary came to the door. "Will you please call Olivia MacDougal to the office?" She nodded and turned to go. Dr. Guess waggled his forefinger at Pria and Ebony. "This would have been very impressive on a college transcript, you know," he chided them. "I hope you girls have thought long and hard about what you are doing."

And that was when it happened.

Ivory stood up, holding her book bag in one hand. "Oh, good Christ—what now?" Dr. Guess muttered.

"Dr. Guess," Ivory said. "You won't be needing a new literature team member. But you do need a science one."

I looked at Peter in confusion. Were Ivory and Ebony having some fight about who could be on the Big Think team? Maybe they had some rule that only one of them could compete in something at one time. (That was weird, but I'd heard of families doing weirder things with twins.) Right now, though, it seemed like both of them were trying to flee the team like a pack of hungry wolverines were approaching the office with tongues wagging.

Was that why Ivory had seemed so cold today? Maybe she had just been fighting with her sister. Maybe—I hoped—it hadn't had anything to do with me at all.

Peter was stroking his chin. He didn't look confused—he looked thoughtful, like he'd suddenly just figured something out. I took the opportunity to lean across and whisper to him. "Do you know what's going on?" I asked. Ebony and Ivory were in some kind of mortal eye lock while Dr. Guess looked perplexed and tapped his pencil angrily.

"I'm not *sure*," Peter said, "but I think—"

Ivory interrupted him. "Dr. Guess, I have a confession," she said. "Ivory and I—played a small

prank. But it seems to have had a lot more conse-
quences than either of us expected."

Dr. Guess shook his head—he wasn't too
swift. But then, neither was I—why was Ivory
referring to herself in the third person? "Ivory,
what are you talking about? What prank?" Dr.
Guess said, each word exiting with its own angry
puff of air.

The office was getting really hot.

Ivory shook her head. "I'm not Ivory," she said.
Then she turned around to face me. "I'm Ebony,"
she said.

I could only look at her dumbly, like a statue
with stone eyes.

"Girls, this is highly unacceptable. How long
have you been doing this?" Dr. Guess snapped.
"Who is the high scorer in literature? Who is involved with the school play? Will someone please
tell me what is going on?" he barked.

Ivory—or was it Ebony?—raised her hand. "It
was just a stupid trick," she broke out. "We didn't
mean anything by it!"

A hot wave began to rise in my chest.

Ebony—or was it Ivory?—shrugged. "It was just
for one day, Dr. Guess. But then when Barry gave
me the lead in the school play, it confused everything. I only did it because Charles—"

So the terrible feeling I was starting to get in my
gut was right. It *had* been about me.

I looked at Ebony. "You're Ivory," I said. The
girl with the curly hair nodded once, coldly.

I looked at Ivory. "And you're Ebony," I said. Behind her glasses and now straggly hair, I could see the eyes of the girl I'd taken to the movies last night.

"And I'm outta here," I said. I stood up, grabbing my backpack, and pounded out of the office. On my way out I almost ran Olivia down—she looked at me with wide eyes, and I muttered, "Sorry."

I had been scorned at schools before, but no one had ever been so mean as to play a *prank* on me *designed* to ensure total humiliation. I couldn't believe it. Everything that I had thought about "Ivory" was wrong. Everything I had thought about this dumb school was wrong.

Ivory had hired her *sister* to play *her*—just to get away from me?

To: Pebbles507@aol.com
From: CoreyFlakes@erols.com

Dear Mary Claire,
    You're never going to believe what's happening.
    You thought the past couple of days were exciting. Well, I have a big, huge heap of "exciting" things to tell you now. I'm so mad, I almost can't even write—it's like the bile is coming up in my throat too fast or something.

Remember Ivory? The great Ivory? The girl who we thought was so mean, then seemed so nice? The girl who was going to be my new friend here? Maybe even—although it makes me just want to laugh to even think how stupid I was about the whole thing now—my girlfriend?

Get this: it was all a big trick.

That's right, ladies and gentlemen. Charles Corey is once again the big dork that everyone has to make fun of.

Honestly, though, Mary Claire—I never really thought anyone would need to do anything this disgusting to me. I can't believe I didn't suspect anything. I can't believe I didn't know from the beginning that it was too weird—and too good—to be true.

I've pretty much figured out exactly what happened, I think.

Ivory hated me, right? But her plan to keep me off the Big Think team didn't work. So she found another way to humiliate me.

This is where the plan gets a little hazy, but I think this was the general idea: Ivory (actually her sister, Ebony) was going to make me get a big crush on her—and convince me that she had a big crush on me. Then she was going to dump me in some really humiliating way so that I left Big Think because I couldn't stand to see her.

What's ironic is that it's Ivory—the real Ivory—who evidently just got the lead in the school play, even though it's her sister—Ebony—who everyone thought was the big actress. So it turns out that she really didn't need her sister to "act" her at all—she probably could have done it herself in a second!

If she could have kept a straight face for a couple of days.

What humiliates me the most is that even though it's such a stupid plan, it worked out so well. I mean, I totally fell for Ivory—I mean, Ebony. I guess they must have known that a guy like me doesn't exactly have girls banging down his door.

Unless they're girls with an ax to grind.

What makes me really worried, though, is that somehow Peter also knew about the whole thing. That everyone has been on this plan to play fool the dork ever since I came to this school. That I've been even more of a laughingstock than I usually am.

Well, it doesn't matter. Because you
know what I'm going to do? I'm going
to tell my parents that there's no
way—no way—that I'm stepping foot anywhere near that school—or anyone who
goes to it—for the rest of the year.
Then I'm going to find something fun
to do this summer—some bike trip or
something.

And I'm going to send Rush Creek a
big fat letter that says they'll be
seeing me in September.

Charles

I hit send and looked at the clock. It was two-
thirty, and Mary Claire would be getting home
soon. Then I laughed. I guess I had done my first
official "cut."

Somehow I didn't think Dr. Guess was going to
be too mad about it. Not that it really mattered
anymore if he was anyway.

Suddenly an IM blinked up on the screen. It was
Peter. I looked at it with dread, wondering if I
should even bother to answer it.

Penrightman: Charles, are you there?
Penrightman: Charles?

Curiosity finally won out. I didn't know
whether Peter had anything to do with what had
happened, after all. And he had been a good

167

enough friend to me—I thought—that it was
worth it to me to find out.

CoreyFlakes: Hey.
Penrightman: I'm glad you're there,
              man. Are you all right?
CoreyFlakes: Not really.
Penrightman: We should talk. Actually,
              not me and you—you and
              somebody else.
CoreyFlakes: So I guess Ivory really
              got back at me for taking
              her place at Big Think,
              huh? I can't believe I was
              so stupid.
Penrightman: That's not how it happened,
              Charles! I was worried you
              were thinking that—but
              that's not how it is.
CoreyFlakes: How is it?
Penrightman: I can't explain. Just meet
              me at Stewart's and I'll
              tell you everything I
              know, I promise. It's not
              what you think, though.
              It's really not, man.
CoreyFlakes: Why can't you just tell me
              this way?
Penrightman: I told you I can't explain.
              Just do me a favor—get over
              to Stewart's, will you?

168

CoreyFlakes: Do I have to?
Penrightman: You have to!!!

I switched off the computer. I wasn't looking forward to whatever was waiting for me at Stewart's.

Thirteen

Ebony

AFTER CHARLES LEFT Dr. Guess's office, chaos broke out.

First Dr. Guess made Pria, Olivia, Peter, and Lucas leave. He turned to us. "Girls," he began, and gave us the biggest tongue-lashing I've ever gotten, outside of the time Ivory and I took our parents' best duvet cover and used it for a picnic blanket in the yard when we were five.

By the end Ivory had somehow convinced Dr. Guess not to call our parents—I'm not sure how. She'd also made him give up the threat to take her out of the play and me off the Big Think team.

Ivory's really good with adults—especially angry ones.

When we left the office, Olivia and Pria were gone. Peter was still sitting on the bench, though, waiting for us.

"I've got to find Pria," Ivory said anxiously, and ran off.

"I've got to talk to you," I said to Peter.

He nodded slowly. "I thought you might," he said.

I was so relieved, I wanted to cry. Did Peter suspect what had been going on all along?

I took a deep breath. "I need your help," I said.

I had been waiting at Stewart's for about half an hour when Charles finally showed up.

I really hadn't thought that Peter was going to be able to convince him to come. (I wouldn't have!) I knew that whatever damage I'd done to our little flirtation, I wasn't going to be able to undo it—not with a million explanations.

But I was going to try.

Charles approached the table like I was a nuclear reactor with a red whirling light on my forehead. He stopped in front of me, his expression stony. Then he spoke.

"Ebony?" he asked.

I nodded.

He nodded back like that explained everything but didn't sit down. "What is it you wanted to say to me?" he asked, like he could scarcely stand to be in my physical presence. Then he looked away, like the ice cream counter was really fascinating today.

I swallowed any pride I had left. "Charles, please sit down," I said. "I want to explain everything that happened today. And apologize."

Like it hurt his legs to do it, Charles finally creaked down to a sitting position. Then he looked over at the far wall.

Just tell him the truth, Ebony, I told myself. *Just tell him the truth, and let him go.*

"Before you say anything," Charles suddenly said, "I just wanted to let you know that I wasn't going to stay at your stupid school anyway. I was accepted at an arts school yesterday." He looked me in the eyes. "So you and your sister could have just sat on your hands instead of trying to screw me over this way."

My tongue felt three times too large. It really was as bad as I thought—Charles thought that we had switched places to mess around with his life and get him back for being on the Big Think team.

And now he was leaving too.

"Charles, that's not it at all," I said. I needed to explain everything, even though it was too late to fix all of it. Or else it would mean that I not only messed up my life entirely—but that I had made the person I liked best in the world unhappy.

"This is kind of humiliating to explain," I said, shredding sugar packets like a maniac. "But I'm just going to try to do it fast and get it over with it."

I didn't look up to get Charles's reaction to any of this. I couldn't bear to look him in the face.

"The last guy I went out with was kind of a jerk," I said, hating how lame and stupid it all sounded. "So when I . . . saw you, I guess I wanted some way to make sure that you weren't a jerk too.

173

And you were with Ivory all the time doing all that Big Think stuff. So I thought . . . if I could just . . . *be* Ivory for a minute, I could figure out whether it was safe to ask you out." I was so embarrassed that I actually put my face in my hands. "Then everything got all messed up!" I muttered through my fingers.

There was silence from the other end of the table. I peeked through my fingers to look at Charles. He was looking at me, his eyebrows furrowed, as if in deep concentration.

"So I'm sorry, Charles," I said. "I'm a complete idiot, and I understand if you never want to talk to me ever again."

I thought he was going to get up and leave right that minute. I looked down at the tabletop so as not to put him under any extra pressure, then gave in to the massive humiliation and just put my whole head down on the table.

Maybe I would live this down in a million, trillion years.

I almost jumped when he spoke again.

"So, you're an actress, huh?" Charles asked in a surprisingly mild voice. "Was it hard that Ivory got that part in the play?"

I looked up. Charles hadn't left—in fact, he was smiling at me slightly. I felt a little burble of hope. "Yeah," I said in a dry little voice. Was he just going to make fun of me about that too?

"You know, I have all these scripts sitting in my closet," Charles continued. "My friend Mary Claire and I used to film them. You wouldn't be interested in replacing her, would you?"

Suddenly I felt my chest drop out. So he already had a girlfriend—that figured. That was probably why he hadn't kissed me last night.

Charles kept talking, my hopes plummeting more with everything he said. "Mary Claire's really amazing," he said. "We still talk by e-mail all the time. She's a brilliant writer and an amazing actress."

Of course she is! I thought jealously.

"She's a genius." Charles laughed. "I miss her a lot."

I knew that I deserved all of this—every stab. "So she was your girlfriend?" I said sadly, trying not to sound bitter. *Ebony, you will obey everything Dev and Olivia tell you for the rest of your life,* I thought.

Charles laughed again. "Not exactly," he said. "She's only ten years old."

I looked up, surprised. Charles reached across the table and took my hand.

"Made you look," he said, smiling.

I felt a burst of hope. I knew I should just keep my big mouth shut, but I couldn't.

"Charles, can we never mention this again?" I asked, squeezing his palm like it was a lifeline.

Charles laughed and took both my hands in his. He smiled across the table at me.

"Aw, I was kinda hoping I could make fun of you, say, for the next couple of years or so," he said, and leaned across the table to kiss me.

As our lips touched, I suddenly had another thought. "But you're going away to that school!" I cried.

Charles kept his lips on mine. "Only if you switch places on me again," he said between kisses. "Only now I'll definitely be able to tell the difference."

A Comedy of Errors,
Act 13, Scene 31

Enter PETER, a HISTORIAN, followed by OLIVIA, DEV, IVORY, and PRIA, with much ex-altation and waving of hands.

PETER: [*clasps hands with* CHARLES, *a* GENIUS] Everything okay here?

OLIVIA: You guys gave us a scare!

EBONY: [*with dawning suspicion*] Peter, how did you know what was really going on?

PETER: [*with reddening of cheeks*] Oh, I had an inside source. [*Looks toward* OLIVIA, *a* POET] Right?

OLIVIA: [*with reddening of cheeks*] I plead the Fifth.

IVORY: Pria, what was all that stuff about helping some friend with a spe-cial project? Were you just trying to distract Mr. Rosner?

PRIA: Not at all. I do have a special project to help my friend on. And it's going to keep us really busy. [*Looks toward* DEV, *an* ATHLETE]

DEV: [*grins*] Guess who the first recruit
for my football team is!

EBONY: Oh my God. The world has ended.

IVORY: We've mixed friends!

DEV: Shut up. You guys were always so
dumb about that. Why don't you just get
over it and get some ice cream?

PRIA: Yeah. We all could have been
friends this whole time if you hadn't
been so stupid.

EBONY AND IVORY: [*exchange looks, then
shrug.* EBONY *hands* DEV *five silver coins*]

EBONY: Mint chocolate chip, all right?

IVORY: Butter pecan. With sprinkles. And
make it snappy!

Do you ever wonder about falling in love? About members of the opposite sex? Do you need a little friendly advice but have no one to turn to? Well, that's where we come in . . . Jenny and Jake. Send us those questions you're dying to ask, and we'll give you the straight scoop on life and love.

DEAR JAKE

Q: *Do guys like when girls wear makeup? A lot of guys say they hate makeup, but I look really bad without it. So what am I supposed to do?*

JJ, New York, NY

A: I'll bet that you don't look really bad without makeup. In fact, I'll bet you look pretty great without a stitch of makeup on! Look, there's nothing wrong with enhancing your features with a little makeup. What guys don't like is a faceful of the stuff: skin covered in foundation, lots of eyeliner and mascara, and ugh: a lot of gooey lipstick.

Q: *Why does my new boyfriend totally ignore me when his friends are around?*

KA, Oak Park, IL

A: It's sort of a guy thing. I'm not saying it's right, but it's something guys seem to do. Sometimes guys don't want their buds to see them fawning all over a girl, so guys will act like they don't care about a girl as much as they really do. If your guy acts like a jerk to you in front of his friends, that's another story, and you need to have a major convo with him about it. But if he's just sort of quiet and doesn't pay a ton of attention to you, he's probably just being a guy.

DEAR JENNY

Q: *I'm seriously crushing on a guy in my English class. He's a brain, though, and I'm considered a total airhead. And brains like brains, right? How can I act smarter?*

MC, Mesa, AZ

A: The best way to get someone to like you, especially someone who's very different from you, is to be yourself. Sometimes it's our very *differentness* that makes us attractive to someone else. Granted, the smartest guy in school is probably not going to like the biggest airhead. But what makes someone an airhead isn't a lack of intelligence. Brains pay attention and listen. Airheads tend to be thinking of everything but what they're supposed to be focusing on, whether a class discussion or a conversation between buds. If you want to change, just try listening. You'll be amazed what you learn!

Q: *Guys never check me out when I walk down the halls. And not one guy in my school has a crush on me. My friend thinks I should start dressing and acting sexier. What do you think?*

TB, Monticello, NY

A: Short skirts and a tight shirt have been known to snag a guy's attention, but—and there's a big *but* coming—sexy clothes and a ton of lip gloss won't keep his attention. The only thing that really will is who you are: your personality. Show the guys of your school who you are *inside*.

Do you have any questions about love?
Although we can't respond individually to your letters,
you just might find your questions answered in our column.

Write to:
Jenny Burgess or Jake Korman
c/o 17th Street Productions,
an Alloy Online, Inc. company.
151 West 26th Street
New York, NY 10001

Don't miss any of the books in *Love Stories* —the romantic series from Bantam Books!